I0624728

Verna and Other Short Stories

Gerry Pratt

This is a work of fiction. Names, characters, places, and incidents either are the product of the author's imagination or are used fictitiously. Any resemblance to actual persons, living or dead, events, or locales is entirely coincidental.

Cover photo by Mark Pratt.

Publisher's Cataloging in Publication
Pratt, Gerry
Verna and other short stories / Gerry Pratt
p.   cm.
ISBN-13: 978-0-615871288

Table of Contents

Arrival

"And what do you do?"

"I'm a newspaperman." To say I was 'in the newspaper business' would imply I know something about the business, the advertising, circulation, paper cost. I know about baseball box scores, the codes on the police radio, deadlines, and the pride in a story with an eight-column banner; enough to know nobody in the newsroom ever yells 'Boy' for a copy kid like Cary Grant in *The Front Page*.

The man seemed satisfied, answering with a nod. But after a minute he turns to examine me more closely. "What paper are you with?"

"I'm going to Portland looking for a job."

"Oh." His expression changed. Maybe he thinks unemployment is catching.

The Seattle train rattles on for a while without our speaking, the Puget Sound flashing past, giving way to meaningless fields of second-growth timber and stump-studded pasture.

The man begins fussing with his briefcase, probably wishing he had sat somewhere else. Finally he turns his head, a furtive, mouse-shaped skull with slick gray hair cropped close above the ears, and offers me his card.

He studies me intently, undecided about something. "My name is Robert Bissell. Bissell? The carpet sweepers? But that's not me. Distant relatives, maybe. I'm the Northwest executive secretary for Regional Canned Goods. You heard of us?"

"No."

"The Oregonian, eh? Fine paper. We read it clear up in Tacoma. That where you are going? The Oregonian?"

"I'm going anywhere I can find a job."

"Well, I am staying at the Multnomah Hotel. If you don't know the town, why don't you check in there. It's the best hotel in town. Maybe I can help you find what you are looking for."

I am certain the man is not gay. He's got a penny-pinching, wouldn't-dare-do-anything-that-might-threaten-the-reputation look about him, and the manner of the organizational worm wiggling his way up by being absolutely nothing, unnoticed, non-threatening. Now he's suddenly out here on the road with an expense account and a room reservation at the best hotel in town.

"No thanks. I'm staying at the Y." I'm tempted to tell him I have six dollars and twenty-five cents in my pocket and two kids at home, but I sense he is already worrying I might end up costing him a cup of coffee or worse, dinner.

When we get off the train he turns away, grip in hand, suddenly an absolute stranger hurrying toward the taxi stand. And I curse myself for believing I could read another man's thoughts. He probably wasn't thinking anything of the kind.

I should have told him I'd just been canned from The Seattle Times copy desk because I misspelled Syracuse. If I meet him again, I will apologize, I promise.

###

Verna

The pale-skinned girl stood in the stern of the small, white ferryboat, a winter breeze kissing her face and tossing her hair into long, wild ribbons of twisting honey. She turned toward me with what I can only describe as a mystical look, with far-away, dreamlike gray eyes that brightened the moment she smiled. It was as if seeing me had somehow awakened a pleasant memory. As long as I remember anything, I shall remember the look, so sensitively beautiful, yet fragile.

She smiled and moved to make room for me at the railing of the ferryboat. I came up beside her and asked if she knew where the boat was scheduled to call. She said she didn't know and she didn't really care. She said she was escaping for the afternoon. I wanted to ask what it was she was escaping, but something about the carefree way she had spoken told me to leave it there. It was an all day cruise, up the Sound, half a dozen ports of call, then back to the city. I had the feeling she had been standing there in the bow ever since we left the wharf.

"My name is Verna," she said, pausing for me to tell her mine.

"Mine is Russo," I said, and she smiled again, full, warm lips parting over even, picture-perfect teeth. She was so physically perfect, yet cool and quietly fragile, like some special ornament taken from a Christmas tree.

"That's a nice, strong name," she said.

"Italian," I answered.

We stood in the wind without talking, watching the wake of the ferry stirring the dark green water into a vanishing trail, disappearing in long, rolling waves. We docked on an island off the north shore of the Sound. Then I asked her. "Shall we get off for a while? Have a walk together. We have some time until the boat leaves."

She said yes, and the boatman opened a section of the railing for us to pass through.

"How long will it be before you leave?" I asked him.

"Half hour," he said. "Better make it twenty-five minutes. You miss this boat and the next run is at four."

"What's there to see here?"

"Never set foot in the place," the boatman said and hurried us through the gate in the railing. I almost stumbled into the water, caught myself about to curse, and then stopped to look at her legs and her body as she stepped off. "You are very beautiful," I said. Even as she took my arm and looked up into my face, she seemed so far away.

"Come on," she said, pushing her head and shoulders forward eagerly. We started up the wharf toward the narrow, dirt road that curved over a rise and into the trees. Beyond the crest of the hill we came upon a store set beside the road with an open-bed truck parked in front. There was a gasoline pump out front and the dark, small store windows were filled with cardboard advertisements for Players Cigarettes and Coca Cola.

"You hungry?"

"Yes," she said. The afternoon wind carried a chill off the water and she pulled her sweater close to her throat with her free hand and pressed her shoulder against my body to block out the wind. A bell suspended over the door to the store dingled as we went in and dingled again as the door shut behind us. Inside, the air was heavy with the scent of stale cereal, coffee grinds and coal oil and damp wood. A heavy-set woman in what looked like a soiled cocktail dress sat reading a newspaper behind the counter. She looked up.

"Good afternoon," she said, putting her paper down.

"We would like something to eat," I said. There was a sparse scattering of cans across the shelves behind the counter and three loaves of wrapped bread in a glass case. A rack for candy bars and cigarettes stood almost empty beside the cash register and several wooden cases of empty soda pop bottles stood stacked by the door.

"We don't have food like that here," the woman said. "Less you want cookies or candy?"

We looked at the sugar cookies. "How about some apples and some cheese?"

"No apples. Can let you have some cheese." The woman shifted her hips heavily from the stool and went to the end of the counter where there was a half round of cheese beneath a plastic cover.

"How much do you want?"

"About fifty cents' worth, make it a dollar," I said.

She began pushing a heavy wooden-handled knife into the cheese, picking up each slice with her pink-polished fingernails and dropping the cheese onto a sheet of wax paper. She folded the paper and handed it to me without weighing. "No apples," she said again. "You might find a few up the hill. People back there sell 'em by the road to the tourists in summer."

"I'll take some smokes too, please. Players," I said. "Large."

She placed the cigarettes on the counter.

"That be all?" I nodded and she wrote the amount of the cheese and the cigarettes on a piece of wrapping paper, a dollar for the cheese, eighty-five cents for the smokes, drew a pencil line below the figures and totaled them. "One dollar and eighty-five cents." She looked up at me like a child who had solved a fourth-grade math problem. I gave her two dollar bills and she went into the back of the store and returned with my fifteen cents. Verna took my arm tightly and began pulling me toward the door like an excited child seeking adventure.

"I want to try for the apples up the road," she said. We went out beneath the dingling bell and she began steering me toward the road leading to the hill and into the trees. When I glanced back at the ferryboat, the wind was kicking small whitecaps up onto the wharf and heavy clouds had moved in from the mouth of the Sound. The road wound behind the store and we stopped in the lee of the building while I cupped my hands over a match to light my cigarette. As an afterthought, I brought the package from my pocket again and offered one to Verna.

"Thank you," she said and put the cigarette in her mouth. I touched my lighted cigarette to hers until she had pulled the life from mine to hers and then we kissed one another on the cheek, on the neck and for a long time on the lips as if it had been a natural ceremony to follow the lighting of our cigarettes. I sensed then that I had kissed her before. It was as if I had kissed her many times and to do it once more was to repeat a long established joy. She laughed and turned her head away and started again toward the hill.

"We may miss the ferry," I said.

"Yes," she answered. But she didn't hurry, nor did I.

"I feel I know you from somewhere," I said. "Have we ever met? Do I know you?"

She shook her head as if to tease me.

"Do you know me?" I asked. "Did you ever know me?"

She shook her head again. "I have not been here for long," she said seriously.

"I'm old enough to be your father."

"I'd like that," she said. "Then I would call you poppa. I like everything about you. I like being here with you. Can I have some cheese?"

"Say cheese," I said.

"Cheese." She mocked the photographer's demand for a posed smile. "Cheese, please. Does it look better when I wet my lips? Cheese."

I unfolded the wax paper and we began eating the cheese as we walked.

The orchard lay in a field that stood beyond a deep roadside ditch. A few pale, yellow apples remained in the naked branches exposed against the gray sky. There was no sign of a house and I jumped across the ditch, landing on my hands and knees in the dry grass. "I'll catch you," I said and she stepped back into the road and jumped after me, falling down on the grass. When I reached to pull her up the bank she was laughing and we fell together.

"You promised to catch me."

"But you didn't come far enough. You should have jumped farther." And we both laughed again as we sat side by side on the shoulder of the ditch.

"It's good to laugh," I said.

"You looked so quiet on the ferry," she said.

"So did you."

"Yes. It made me sad to see you looking like that," she answered. "Are you still sad?"

"Yes. But it doesn't mean a hell of a lot to you," I said. And I was sorry the moment the words had passed my lips. "What I meant is, it's not anything for you to worry about." Even that sounded bad when I said it, but I decided to leave it there.

"That's wrong," she said. "When you are happy, you should share happiness. Like we are now. When you are sad, it touches other people the same way. It made me sad just to see you sad."

"You are right, I know. It's just that I have been feeling sorry for myself for a long time and..." I shrugged, hoping that would end things.

She looked up from the grass into my eyes, reaching with her hand to trace my cheek and chin with her fingers. "You are good looking," she said. "Nice hair. You have the look of someone who could do anything he wanted to do. That's right, isn't it?"

"I can buy my own drinks, if that's what you mean."

"Can you buy me an apple?"

"That's supposed to be your job, isn't it?"

She looked about in mock astonishment and laughed. "I pick the apple, you eat it? Is that it? And this is the Garden of Eden?"

"Well, the orchard may be a little worse for wear, but you have to admit it's nice here. It's quiet and out of the wind and you are here. Who's to say this isn't the place?"

"Okay." She jumped to her feet. "You sit there." She went into the orchard and picked two of the remaining apples and brought them back to me. They were hard, thick-skinned and sweet and we ate them with the rest of the cheese. From across the hill we could hear the shrill call of the departing ferryboat and went on eating the apples.

"I remember a girl in my life who once told me that if you didn't ask a lot from God, then God stopped offering and stopped giving. She believed it and I began to believe it for awhile."

"Is she the reason you have been so sad?"

"Yes, in the beginning. Though now there are only bits and pieces left for me to remember when I try to talk about it. The memories are all mixed up with pressed flowers that lost their color in the pages of a book, and her ink-stained letters that I have never read and lockets with miniature pictures that have begun to look like pictures of strangers to me."

"Tell me about her."

"We missed the ferry you know."

"Yes. So you have time now. Tell me."

"No," I said. "I have stopped telling people. There was a time when I sat in bars and told strangers. That's how I came to realize nobody really gives a damn. It doesn't mean anything to anybody else. Donne wrote that no man is an island; each is part of the main. He was wrong. We are all islands, isolated and alone. We are born and we die alone. We live our single moment in time, solo flights, beginning and ending. Always alone."

As I repeated some of the words I had used so often before, a vision of the fat doctor passed before me in the apple orchard. And I could see beyond Verna's gray eyes, beyond the dead grass and the naked apple trees. His face was unchanged.

"There really is no point in telling," I said and heard my own voice trailing off in protest as the story began once more. "It's all buried somewhere in the attic of my mind. I can remember there was a silver mug with her name on it and a wallet they brought to me that day, a wallet stuffed with all the brick-a-brack precious to a teenager. I barely looked, but I knew there were a couple of love letters and some mushy writing on photographs of dizzy looking boys with high school haircuts, like they used to wear."

The wind caught the corner of the field and chased the dried leaves up the side of the bank, bringing my thoughts back to the orchard. "That's all there is," I said. "That and a rose-colored marble headstone with her name in a cemetery on a hill, her name and an inscription I saw written in a child's poetry book when I was running away. It says, 'Beauty Seen Is Never Lost.' The dates are there too, April 1, 1953, and September 18, 1969. That's how long she lived. Sixteen years."

Verna sat quietly waiting for me to go on.

"She was born in Toronto. We were too young to have babies, but we made love a lot and we got pregnant. It was as if we were being punished for loving so much. We were both working, paying for a ten-year-old Studebaker on time. We tried hot baths because somebody told us that would bring on her period. Then she tried jumping off the toilet onto the bathroom floor, barefoot. We even tried Milk of Magnesia. Nothing worked. All we did was make the people in the apartment downstairs sore because of all the noise from jumping off the toilet."

Even as I talked, trying to hold back the words, trying to cut short the story, it played back again like a very old movie that flicks and stops with the voices coming in staccato, high-pitched sounds. But the words the voices spoke were unchanged and clear.

***

"Russo, nothing works." She was frightened.

"What the hell," I said. "We gotta go see a doctor. Maybe it's a tumor or something. Maybe it is not a baby and we have done all this for nothing."

He was a fat doctor with damp, sweaty hands and a receding chin but he had good eyes and smiled quickly when we told him we thought we were pregnant. "You wait out here and read a magazine or something," he said to me and called his nurse into the examining room. I was reading a National Geographic on Niagara Falls when he came out and closed the door behind him. "She's three, maybe four months pregnant," he said. "She's just a little tyke. We have to be very careful. Have you been careful?"

"No," I said, "we haven't been careful. We have been jumping off the toilet seat. We have been soaking in hot baths, she has I mean. She even took salts and Milk of Magnesia so she would have her period. We didn't want a baby. We are not sure of anything yet. We are too young." It embarrassed me to talk to him like that, but he had good eyes and I was afraid we had hurt her. He had to know it all.

The laughter, the paternal goodwill, left his eyes and suddenly he looked older and even fatter than he did before. "What a lot of crap," he sighed and said nothing for a minute. "Where do you kids pick up all this bullshit? Why didn't you think of that when you were so busy screwing?" He looked exasperated. "She could be in trouble," he said. "She's so damn tiny. I can't really tell yet. Why the hell don't you grow up and enjoy being pregnant? It's the first time for you, isn't it? Sure it is and it's certainly the first time for that narrow-assed little girl of yours. Now can be the best time of your life, if you grow up," he said and turned back into the examining room.

She bought Chinese smocks and tight-fitting black leotards with the belly cut out of them so they would fit and she tried to be sexy all of the time. I remember getting horny every time I saw her belly and she bought sheer night gowns so that she looked huge and solid in them and she pushed it against me at night and we mad love even after the fat doctor told us not to do it anymore. She had to. It scared her to be so big and she had to know it was still there working good for her and I had to prove it to her, but I wanted to, all of the time.

God it was a red-faced baby. I sat in the hospital room holding her hands while she was in labor and I hated it, I hated myself and I hated her too. It began in the morning and she was yelling all of the time.

"You better get out of here," the doctor told me about ten o'clock that night. He ordered the nurse to take her away where they could try to stop her hurting so much. At twelve o'clock, I have always said it was twelve, I never did know what time it was, only that I had been sitting on the slippery red plastic chair for hours when the fat doctor came and stood over my chair in the waiting room. He put his hand on the chrome arm of the chair like he was supporting himself so he wouldn't fall on his face. I looked up, trying to bring myself erect on the slippery cushion. He lifted his thick, damp hand and placed it on my shoulder. "We lost her," he said.

He had his surgical mask pulled down beneath his chin. I thought he was crying. "She was having a helluva time. We gave her anesthetic and she just stopped breathing. We lost her."

"What do you mean you lost her?" I still didn't understand what he was saying. He wasn't making sense.

"We did a helluva lot to try and save her. The anesthesiologist did things. God, I took her heart in my hand trying." His large head swayed helplessly from side to side. "She was just worn out. There was nothing left. She was so damn tiny. Damn. She's dead. Your lady is dead," he said. I began to sink onto the red plastic chair. It was bottomless and I was going down.

"You son of a bitch," I said. "You rotten son of a bitch." I didn't know if I was talking to him or myself. "I don't believe you." But I did and then I screamed. I screamed as loud as I could because I couldn't hold what it was that was happening inside me. There were a couple of nurses who came up then and one sat down beside me.

"Shh. Shh. There are sick people sleeping here. Stop that. Control yourself." I heard what she said and heard myself scream again. "Get him something," the nurse said. The doctor just stood there, his head going from side to side. Then another guy in a surgical gown came up with his cap on. There was blood all over his front.

"What's happening? Jheesus. Is this her husband?"

The nurse told him. "We have to do something before he yells the whole ward down." But I stopped screaming. It hurt more when I screamed so I stopped. I was only interested in my own pain.

"Where is she?" I heard myself ask like it was coming out in printed words, slow and flat.

"They are taking her downstairs," the other guy in the surgical gown and cap said. He had a paper cup of water and some blue and white pills. "Here," he said, and I swallowed the pills and drank the water.

"I want to go with her," I said and stood up.

"You have a baby girl," the fat doctor said.

I stared at him trying not to hear what it was he was saying. "I don't want to hear that. I don't want to listen to you," I said.

"We saved the baby. It's a girl," he said.

Then I saw her; I saw the red, red face all squeezed together. They had her wrapped in a blanket and I remember thinking her face was so red because of the blood but it wasn't blood. She was just very red with a lick of black hair coming down onto her forehead. She looked like a wicked nun, roasted so that her face was wreathed in pain and her skin boiled red.

I shook my head at him. "I don't want to see that. I don't want to see that." I turned away and pushed toward the room where they said she died.

"You can't go in there. They are cleaning up in there. Don't do that to yourself," the second doctor said. I stopped. "Come with me. We can get some coffee and talk, then I will take you to her downstairs." He motioned for the nurse to take the baby away. It was chuckling and choking, making urgent mouthing gasps at life and in that instant I was aware of her being alive. "She came by cesarean. It was after we lost her mother," the second doctor said. "Just don't think of that right now."

He pulled off his surgical cap and his mask and wrapped them in his bloodied smock and handed it all to one of the nurses. Underneath he was wearing a collarless green shirt with short sleeves and sack-like trousers cinched at the waist with a drawstring. He was very young and his hair was curly and long and he wore paper sacks over his shoes. "It's tough," he said. "But we should talk about it." He gave me a cigarette as we went to the elevator. The pills had begun to work and I felt the floor dropping away.

"I'm going to be sick," I said.

"That will pass in a minute," the young doctor said. "Breathe deeply and relax. It will pass."

We drank coffee without saying anything for a while and then he asked me. "Is there anything you want to know? How it happened? What we did? There will have to be a hospital hearing and there will be a post mortem report, with your permission. The hospital would really appreciate that. It would help us all."

"Go to hell. Your partner said you already cut her open. He told me he held her heart in his hand."

"We both did," the young doctor said. "She just didn't want to come back."

"No post mortem. Just give her back to me."

"We can't do that."

"Like hell you can't. I'm taking her out of here tonight."

"Ok." He placed his hands on the table and stood up and signaled to the guy who was attending the coffee urns in the cafeteria. I didn't listen to what they said, but the other guy sat down with me when the doctor left.

"Is there anybody we can call to come down?" the cafeteria guy asked.

"No. We are from the West Coast. We don't have any relatives. Is that what you mean?"

"How about friends?"

I shook my head. "I don't feel like talking anymore. Leave me alone. I don't want to talk anymore."

"Sure. That's all right," he said and got up and went back behind the food trays.

When the young doctor came back he was smoking again, taking long nervous drags on his cigarette. The fat doctor was with him. "Her body is in emergency downstairs," the young guy said. "Doctor Smith called a mortuary. You can pick any one you want tomorrow, so don't worry. You are not bound to the people coming tonight. If you want, you can accompany the body to the mortuary when they come for her. Is that what you want?"

"Yes. I want to see her now."

"Russo. That's your name, isn't it?" he said. I didn't answer. He looked at the fat doctor.

"You are emotionally upset, kid," the fat doctor said. "I don't want you to see her tonight. Wait until tomorrow. You are very tired now and when you are tired you can't control your emotions. That screaming upstairs was very bad."

I accepted that and shook my head.

After a while they took me down to the emergency where I sat on a wooden bench in the hall between the two of them, waiting for the undertakers to come for her body. As we sat there, the hospital public address system chimed softly and a woman's voice came on, praying in Latin. It was a gentle-sounding prayer and it floated through the entire hospital and I knew it was a nun praying for the dead. I thought then that there were people who would know someone else had died. I thought that must scare the hell out of sick people. I remembered the times I thought I had been dying, when there had been blood in my shit, and the time when I thought I couldn't swim back to the boat in the lake. I chuckled and started to laugh out loud. The young doctor held my hand.

"Those pills are pretty strong pills, young fellow. Take it easy on yourself for awhile."

I didn't see the men from the undertaking parlor go in but two of them came up to the bench. "We have the body outside," one of them said to me. "Do you want to ride with the hearse?"

"No. No, I don't think so," I said.

The man from the funeral parlor handed the fat doctor a card and the doctor gave it to me. "She will be there until you decide," he said. "Call them when you are ready. We can take care of the baby until you have a chance to sort things out. The baby should be in the hospital a week or more anyway. It was tough for her too. That's a blessing you know, the child."

I wanted to spit on him but I merely nodded. "Thanks. Doc, do you think it was all the things we did to kill the baby when she was pregnant?"

"Christ no. She was just very small and she was living with what we believe was a damaged heart. Probably rheumatic fever when she was young, when she was a child," he said. "We won't know that for sure unless there is an autopsy."

The young doctor touched the fat doctor's arm. "We have already discussed that," he said. "He doesn't want to decide anything tonight."

The noise that had been exploding inside of me had begun to settle quietly into a morbid complacency and while I heard them and looked at their anxious faces, it didn't seem real anymore. Nothing did.

"Let us arrange for someone to drive you home," the young doctor said.

"No. We have a car," I said. "I drove her here in it, if it's still out there. I am okay now."

"You sure?"

"I'm okay," I insisted. I got to my feet and went past them toward the ambulance doors. There were two automatic doors leading outside. The first one opened with a buzzing noise when I stepped on the rubber exit mat. I turned in the chamber between the two doors to look back at the doctors. They were gone and I went outside into the dark. Our Studebaker was parked against the curb up the block and I started toward it, walking with one hand on the hospital wall. Then I stopped and pressed my face against the bricks and slowly, deliberately, began to beat my head against the bricks.

***

The wind had found us in the orchard grass and its stirring through the naked apple branches brought me back again to Verna's gray eyes watching intently as I pulled my hand over my face. My head had begun aching hard again and I stood up, pulling her to her feet. The afternoon sky had grown dark and the trees were merely shadows fading into the open field. "Come on," I said, "or we will be here all night."

She stood up. "What about the baby?"

"We were not married," I said. "We hadn't even known each other very long. They came to see me about a week later and I signed adoption papers to let her go. I didn't even want to look at her. It was guilt, I guess. I couldn't get past the idea that I had killed her mother. I couldn't handle the looking at her because of all the things we did, because of our lovemaking. I couldn't get it off my back. I hated the baby. It was easier hating the baby than it was hating myself."

She took my arm and we started down the hill into the face of the wind.

"Oh, I got curious after awhile, but not too curious. They told me that if I showed up, I would cause the adopting family all kinds of harm. I would harm the child too. So I dropped it without ever finding out where she was or who she was. Looking back, I guess I never really wanted to find her. I didn't know how I would handle it. I kept trying to explain to her in my mind how it was. How I didn't want to see her even though I was the only person she really had in the whole damn world. I never could figure how to explain that."

"But what about the pictures and the wallet? Those were hers, weren't they?"

I looked into the wide, gray eyes, searching softly for an answer. "Verna, you look cold. Let me give you my jacket," I said. I took it off and put it over her shoulders. The late afternoon chill touched the skin beneath my shirt. The store had closed and we leaned against the side of the building out of the wind. "I took the ferry up here this afternoon to forget all this," I said. "Now I am laying it all on you."

"Did you think you could just sail away and forget her?" she said seriously.

"I could forget a lot of things by going into the water." I felt her tighten her grip on my arm.

"Oh. That frightens me. Why? Why would you do that now? It was a long time ago."

"No. It just began a long time ago. I thought I had gotten rid of it. Turning away from the baby was like taking off a pair of gloves. I was disappearing like those doctors disappeared. I got married a couple of times. But no more kids. I made sure there would be no more kids. And in time, I did get away. It didn't stop hurting, it just drew back inside where

I could smother it. Bury it deep enough and you no longer know it is there eating at you every day."

The back door of the store opened. "You people want to come inside?" It was the lady in the soiled cocktail dress who had sold us the cheese. She had a heavy, hand-knitted cardigan sweater thrown over her shoulders.

"When is the ferry due?" I asked.

"Should be there now," she said and disappeared inside the store.

"Want to go inside?"

"You are cold without your coat," Verna said.

"Not very."

The woman appeared again. "The ferry is coming in now. If you go on down, you can get aboard. You better hurry. It doesn't stay long."

We thanked her and left the protection of the store wall and began running down the dirt road. The small boat was bouncing against the wharf where we had come ashore. Inside the cabin she gave me back my coat.

"Please tell me the rest," she said. "It helps to talk about it. I know it does."

There was a light the size of a large flashlight bulb burning in the ceiling of the closed cabin and we were alone. The railing gate slammed shut outside and the engine picked up as the ferryboat began to work its way back into the channel. I had to raise my voice for her to hear me above the chattering of the engine.

"September 18, 1969, she came back to me," I said. As I spoke, I could feel again the small package settling heavily in my hands, a heavy folded manila envelope with a rubber band bunching it together in a lump. There was a policeman standing at the door.

"Mister Russo?"

"Yes," I said. I didn't like policemen coming to my place. It brought back memories of days when their coming meant other things, when I was drinking a lot. When I hurt people.

"Mister Russo, we have been asked to contact you on behalf of the Ontario Provincial Police. May I come in?"

I opened the door wider and he came inside. "Sit down. Would you like a beer?" I knew he wouldn't take one. I had asked out of perversity as much as courtesy.

"No. You go ahead. I have work to do yet and I don't need people saying I am drinking on duty." I didn't know whether he meant that for me, but I let it pass. He was not being friendly.

"Mister Russo. You are the Michael Russo who lived in Toronto in the early fifties?"

"Yes."

"Father of a child born out of wedlock in fifty-three?"

That scorched. "What the hell is this?"

"Well, that child and her adoptive parents were involved in a boating accident recently. These are the child's belongings." He handed me the package and an official form and a telegram. "There is a lawyer in Ontario who wants you to call. It seems the girl, her parents, five people in all, were all drowned. There were instructions from the parents that you were to be notified. Apparently it was part of their final arrangements in case something like this happened to both of them. The lawyer said they arranged that if they both died, you, as the natural father, were to be appointed guardian. The girl outlived them by a matter of hours, I believe."

I took the rubber band off the envelope. The policeman was a blank. He was a voice. I couldn't tell you then or now what he looked like, only that he came in a uniform and that he sat there throwing hard balls that were landing inside my head. "Their name was Wright, Mr. and Mrs. Joel Wright," he said. "The telegram is from their attorney, the one who is handling the estate. If you will sign the receipt for the goods, Mister Russo, I will be on my way."

"Sure," I said. I took his ballpoint pen and signed the form on my knee without reading it.

"There was no money in the wallet," the policeman said as he got up to leave. He let himself out the door.

It was a soft, worn, red leather wallet. It had been soaked in water and stuck together so that it wouldn't open easily. I laid it on the table and dumped out the manila envelope. I got as far as opening the two lockets, they were good quality and each carried a picture of a girl who looked so much like her mother that the picture never leaves me. Her hair is tied back in a ponytail, her face wearing a soft, vulnerable smile. The letters, two of them, were creased and folded hard so the edges had broken with age. They were love letters from boys.

It was raining when the lights of the city began to appear. Verna let go of my hand. I lit a cigarette and handed it to her. "They said she was mine, and then she was dead and she was mine. So I flew to Toronto and buried her on a hill. Now you know all about me."

"Yes," she said. She looked at the watch on my wrist, lifting my hand to see the dial in the dim light. "Do you know it is after eight o'clock?"

"I didn't notice anything to do with time today," I said. "Where are you going now?"

"I have an appointment to keep," she said.

"When can we meet again?"

"I am not sure we can."

"Please. Tell me where I can reach you."

"I'm only here for a short while and I'm not free," she said.

"You mean you are married?" I looked at her ring finger. It was bare.

"Not exactly, but something like that," she said.

"If I can't call you, will you meet me again?"

She looked puzzled, pained it seemed. "I will try," she said.

"Please. I want very much to see you again. There are things we have not yet put together. I don't know how to say it, but it's important, very important we see each other, at least once more."

The boat docked and the deck hand opened the door to the cabin and told us to get off.

"I'll be here. The same ferry tomorrow," I said. "Will you come? Even if you can't make the trip, come to the ferry."

She kissed me again, on the cheeks, and on the mouth quickly. I squeezed my fingers through the loose knit of her sweater, afraid to let her go. We walked together to the taxi stand at the end of the wharf and she left.

Every day that week I rode the same ferry. Now I come in the fall because it's cool and quiet here after the summer rush. The boat doesn't stay long, but if you miss this one, there is another late in the afternoon. No, there is nothing much to see on the island. If you hike up the road a half mile there's an old orchard with hard sweet apples that are worth the hike. But try not to miss the last ferry. It's a long wait if you are alone.

###

An Angel's Garden

Tire tracks broke through the dry grass in parallel paths toward the house that stood on a rise beyond the trees. Staggered sticks and naked vines of a depleted vegetable garden spread out from the path into an uncultivated field so that there was no clean line of where the old lady's work had begun or finished. It was fall and the sun felt soft and delicate in the chill wind, its warmth reaching out like the last words from a departing friend. She stood, strands of her thin gray hair, broken loose from the pins, moving in the wind. "It's too late," she said. "Everything is gone. Come back next summer."

But she didn't turn away. Maybe she was curious in a way old people become curious about young people, maybe she was lonely and thinking there would not be any others to talk to this day. Maybe she was planning to do business all along and this was merely the way she went about it when there wasn't much to sell. The hand-painted sign leaning precariously against the mailbox had said 'cukes, corn, tomatoes, garden fresh.'

"Where you from," she said as if she had the right to know. It was past the summer tourist season, and the young couple dressed in going-away clothes must have presented a curious picture standing in the grass by the road.

"We are on our honeymoon," the boy said and unconsciously let go of the girl's hand. "We are renting a cottage down by Whalen's store in the

Bay." The story in the paper said they had motored south, but the Bay wasn't south, technically it wasn't even across the line. A softness passed through the old lady's eyes and she brushed the hair from her face.

"What did you want?" she said, "I don't have much of anything left."

" It doesn't matter. Is there any corn?" he said.

"We will see," she said and stepped off into the corn patch. There were large brown freckles on the backs of her hands and her small, slim fingers looked as if they had been wrapped in parchment. She sent them expertly thrusting through the rustling corn stalks and began to tear away the ears. "These might be all right," she said and handed the boy the corn. The work had started her breathing harder. "Let's see if there are any decent cukes. Most of them are too big now." She turned and looked at the girl who was wearing a yellow dress and bright brown leather shoes. "You better stay back now. Don't go getting the pretty dress all dirty. I'll bet you are not even twenty, eh?"

"Twenty one," the girl said.

The old lady smiled. "Don't look it. Neither one of you." She pulled the smallest of the cucumbers away from the vines." Now come up to the house and I'll see if I have some ripe tomatoes." She led the way along the tire tracks to the small house with an overturned rowboat leaning against the kitchen wall.

"Your husband a fisherman?" the boy asked.

"No. My man worked in the cannery. He's been

gone a long time now. Before you were born."

The tomatoes were wrapped in newspaper. They had been picked green and wrapped to ripen on the cool porch. She wiped each of them in the skirt of her apron as she handed them to the girl.

"We came here when we were your age," she said as if that were some kind of coincidence and seemed momentarily disappointed they didn't share her amazement. "There now, be on your way," she said and handed the girl the last of the tomatoes.

"How much do we owe you?" the boy said.

"That's my wedding present," the old lady said. "Maybe you will come back next year and I'll let you buy something then. Get on with you now." She walked with them along the tire tracks to the road and stopped to pick two large dahlias from the garden beside the house and handed them to the girl.

"You have a long way to go, young lady," she said. "It's nice if you can have some flowers now and then along the way. You remember to bring her flowers, young fella."

"Ok," the boy said and thanked her and promised they would come next year when the garden was young.

In the cottage the corn was sweet and fresh and the tomatoes, served chilled with drops of water on the firm flesh, were like sun-ripened fruit. They ate them together and made love and invented stories in bed about the angel they had met in the garden on the hill by the road.

###

The Horse With A Message

Perhaps I am stretching things when I claim that a man and a horse can enter each other's minds. I am not talking of a circus horse walking on its hind legs to a ringmaster's whip, nor an Austrian stallion dancing the waltz, nor a racehorse bursting a tendon stretching for the finish in answer to some itinerant jockey's exhortations.

What I'm talking about is an inter-mingling of behavior between man and horse, the kind of reflex communication that develops between a bakery wagon gelding and a hundred-and-twenty-pound Liverpool immigrant feeding a wife and six kids by peddling bread and cakes door to door for a living. I'm talking about the kind of man-to-horse, horse-to-man communication that takes place beneath a farmer's hands as he cradles the heavy leather reins in the crook of his arm and paces off furrow after furrow behind the rump of a tired mare.

What I'm talking about you can see in the purposeful, stoic stance of a policeman's patrol horse resting hip shot at the entrance to the park, its hide quivering like an expectant virgin, sensitive to the slightest signal from the jodhpur-clad legs straddling its back.

Joe Blackburn was assigned the brown gelding his first day at McGavin's Bakery. The name Rex was scratched over the horse's stall, a name Blackburn reasoned had been carved in the beam long before this gelding had ever taken up residence.

He mentally re-christened the beast Brownie, a subtle, familial connection to his own nickname, which was Blackie. At the same time, it was a name with less authority and force than his own, a subordinate in color, as it were. And over time, as if in recognition of his new title and affiliation, Brownie assumed something of the appearance of his large-nosed Liverpool driver, as well as more than a trace of Joe's sardonic personality.

On their very first trip out of the barn, the horse notified Joe in no uncertain terms that there was no room in their relationship for the authority the driver had at first assumed.

"Giddyap," Joe cracked and touched the gelding with the tip of the driver's whip. In the time it takes for a rifle bullet to pass through the barrel of a gun, Brownie farted, a large, lip-quivering blast that Joe would swear hit him squarely in the mouth, leaving a bad taste and the feeling of having been mildly sprayed with something unpleasant.

"Shit," Joe muttered as the horse continued on at its own pace, but not fast enough for Joe. "Giddyap, you bastard," Joe snarled and came down again with the whip on the horse's rump. It was as if he had whacked a hair-trigger machine gun. A second, large burst of gas exploded from the horse's rear, engulfing the entire driver's box in an obnoxious cloud. One more tentative touch with the whip nearly lifted Joe out of the driver's box; the whip went back into the cradle for good.

Once that was out of the way, the relationship became amiable through the remainder of Joe

Blackburn's twenty-odd years of peddling McGavin's bread through the back alleys. The horse learned quickly, stopping and starting without so much as a clicking of the driver's tongue. It got so that Joe never did pick up the reins, even with the ever increasing traffic, which was becoming more and more of a headache for one who grew up with horse-drawn delivery.

When it came time for his last day on the job, Joe was somewhat curious as to whether Brownie's attitude had changed over the years. In a reckless moment, he pulled the whip out of the cradle and landed a sharp whack to Brownie's rump. Without losing a step, Joe swore until his final day, the horse turned its head, looked back at the driver, and smiled.

###

Olivia

It was two weeks before Christmas when Rupert arrived at Molly's house with Olivia, his live-in lady. He had 'borrowed' a Model T truck and announced that he was taking the kids and Olivia to the North Shore for cedar boughs and perhaps a Christmas tree or two to peddle in White Rock. Molly, happy to see her kids being drawn into the Christmas spirit, made them peanut butter sandwiches, then shook her head hopelessly as Rupert, posing at the steering wheel of the Ford with theatrical élan, pulled on a pair of grey pallbearers' gloves while laughing through his broken front teeth. The gloves were a gift of his momma's new-found undertaker friend, Ezra Rozelle.

The Model T was a caricature of a truck with the driver's seat perched over the engine cowling in front of a large, teetering cargo box. The box extended beyond the wheels so that it appeared as if the truck was about to tip back onto its haunches at any moment.

Rupert drove the old crate like he was Barney Oldfield, careening into the North Shore Drive with the throttle wide open, charging up the mountain so that the box shuddered as the truck hit the dirt roads, threatening to shake loose with the kids inside.

A wind-whipped December drizzle slicing across the North Shore drove the four kids to cover beneath a cargo canvas until they felt the truck

stagger to a stop within a tall stand of cedar. Rupert
and Olivia were the first to hit the ground, sizing up
the woods for their point of attack. Between them,
they carried a kitchen knife and an axe, along with
an assortment of saws and clippers for the kids.

By late afternoon, as the lights of the city began
appearing on the far side of the inlet, they had
loaded the Ford with a mountain of wet evergreens.
Dillon and his two sisters were playing at mapping
out the route home by following the chain of
headlights trailing over the Second Narrows Bridge
as Rupert and Olivia tied down the last of the load.

"It's all downhill from here," Rupert announced,
stuffing the last of a sandwich into his mouth. "But I
wanna go back fo juss a minute," he mumbled
thickly, swallowing the last of the peanut butter and
wiping a sleeve across his mouth. "I saw a tree back
there. There's room on top of the load. The kids can
hang on to it. If we can't sell it it'll be right for the
house, eh?" He was adding up the nickels and dimes
of the load.

"Rupert, no. We have enough," Olivia urged,
lurching wearily to her feet, chilled by the prospect
of heading back into the wet underbrush. "Please,"
she pleaded.

"I saw a little man up there in the brush," he
hollered back at her. "Red suit and white whiskers?
He might be the man who has your Christmas
present. You stay by the truck, Ollie."

"Can't we get a tree on another trip?" Olivia
complained.

"Won't have the truck," hollered Rupert over his shoulder, now a mere vanishing shadow of steam disappearing into the trees.

It was a steep embankment and Rupert's muscles felt slack and unresponsive beneath his wet trousers. His soaked overcoat clinging to his shoulders weighed a ton. He heard Olivia stagger up the hillside behind him. She was at his shoulder when he reached the small tree he was after.

Quickly, without finding a secure place to kneel, he dropped to one knee and raised the axe. It felt heavy and awkward in his tired arms as he swung at the supple tree. The blade bounced off the trunk. "God damn. Stand back, Olivia." She reached to steady the trunk. Rupert swung again, a glancing blow that sent the axe flying out of his hands. He picked up the axe and chopped again, savagely. This time the axe slid off the tree, the force of his blow driving the axe blade into the taught muscle of his thigh. Rupert fell back onto the wet earth, dumb with shock as he watched the soft earth soak up his blood.

"Rupert. Good God," Olivia gasped as she dropped to the ground beside him.

"Cheesus Christ alive, Olivia. I cut my God damn leg," he muttered, the blood seeping through his fingers like red grease. He wanted to get up and run and started to tremble. He forced himself to wiggle his toes in his boot to know if the mechanics of his legs were still working. "Oh, Olivia. For God's sake help me," he cried.

Without a word, Olivia slipped out of her heavy
woolen jacket and tried twisting it into a clumsy
tourniquet. Then just as quickly, she stripped off her
thin jersey sweater, her large, naked breasts
punching out into the chill mountain air like brown-
nipple wine skins. She felt the cold raindrops on her
skin as she pulled and twisted the sweater into a
semblance of a cord. Swiftly, she wrapped the
sweater above the cut, the warm, sticky blood
oozing through her fingers.

"You are going to catch your death of cold,"
Rupert whispered, as if he were afraid of being
overheard. He was suddenly uncomfortable with
Olivia's tits out where the entire world could see.
Olivia tried to answer with a smile, busying herself
by slipping the axe handle beneath her makeshift
rope and twisting until the tourniquet drew tight.

'Oh God, Olivia. Easy. Go easy, please" Rupert
shut his eyes momentarily, and when he opened
them she was grinning at him.

"It stopped. The blood has stopped," she said
triumphantly.

"Honey, you saved my life. You saved me from
bleeding to death," Rupert said with the breathless
reverence of a man who had just witnessed a
miracle. He lay back on the ground and looked up at
her with adoration, a look that seemed to remind
him that Olivia was naked from the waist up.

A shudder went through her body as she looked
into his frightened eyes and his pale skin. She was
hot, breathing rapidly, trying to deny the sensuous

urge to fondle him as he lay in her arms. Rupert sensed what was happening.

"Good God, woman. What in hell is the matter with you? I'm hurt. I could be bleeding to death any minute."

"Shh. Hush now." She pressed her mouth to his, her warm, soft-lipped kiss held for a breathless moment before she sat up quickly. "We have to get you out of here before it gets dark."

The shadows of late afternoon were gone with only the dim half-light of early evening revealing the outline of their trail. "Rupert, you are going to make it. I'm going to help you and you are going to make it back to the truck."

Rupert nodded grimly. "I cut through the bark. The tree is going to die. It's worth a buck at least."

"For God's sake, forget the bloody tree." Olivia took Rupert's free arm. Looping the arm over her shoulder, she began pulling him, stumbling through the brush.

As quickly as she had ignited his hope, she sensed Rupert's courage leave when the two of them collapsed alongside the truck. The high-step into the cab was enough to convince him he wasn't going to make it into the cab any more than he was going to be able to drive the Ford off the mountainside.

"How are we going to get outta here?" he whined. "The pedals, the steering. I can't drive with this leg. I can't, Olivia." He was in tears, and from among the bed of cedar in the truck box he could hear Isabelle, the youngest, crying.

"All right. Everybody shut up," Olivia shouted. She pushed and shoved Rupert into the passenger side of the Model T.

"You are going to drive?" Rupert asked meekly. "You don't know how."

"I'll manage," she said, settling him into the cab. Rupert's leg had begun to bleed again and she stopped to tighten the tourniquet.

"Ouch. Jesus Christ, Olivia," Rupert winced, the pain momentarily taking his mind off the hazards of her driving the truck.

"Now, let's get the hell out of here. Everybody hang on up there. And Isabelle, for God's sake stop your bawling."

It had begun raining in earnest, soaking Olivia's dark hair so it hung close to her face, wild and strangely beautiful as she leaned over the Ford radiator, poised over the crank.

"God, we are never going to make it," Rupert wailed as he set the spark and the hand throttle. "Olivia. Watch out for the bloody kick. That crank can break your arm."

"Rupert, shut up," she hollered, the excitement of the moment flashing in her eyes. Bracing one hand on the radiator, she spun the crank. There was no response.

"Easy," Rupert called out. "Don't jerk it."

Again, Olivia dropped her powerful shoulders and spun the crank in a reckless whirl. The engine coughed, then roared to life. Rupert eased off the hand throttle as Olivia jumped into the cab, both hands gripping the steering wheel.

"She's a lot stronger than Rupert," Dillon said, reassuring his sisters. "Olivia can do anything. Just watch. She's going take us and this truck all the way home."

Olivia released the hand brake, turned the front wheels into the road ruts and with Rupert's voice rising with increasing terror, she began to feel the loaded truck come into her hands. "Turn left. Turn right. Slow down, for God's sake!" Rupert continued to holler.

The truck was into the main flow of North Shore traffic when Olivia first realized she was on the causeway funneling into the Second Narrows Bridge. "I have to turn off somewhere and get you to a hospital," she shouted over the engine.

"You want to land me in jail?" Rupert hollered over the engine's roar. "For God's sake, Olivia, you got no license. This damn truck has only one headlight. And if anybody finds out I borrowed it from the service yard, we are all in for car theft." His shouting tapered off as he noticed the road narrowing.

Olivia would have probably spotted the trouble up ahead if Rupert hadn't been shouting in her ear. But her concentration was on the three pedals beneath her feet and her eyes were focused on the wet pavement ahead. She was also struggling to keep the front end of the truck from wandering into the oncoming traffic, the over-loaded rear end all but lifting the front wheels off the road.

It was only when the Ford rolled onto the final bridge approach that she saw the steel superstructure forming a basket-like tunnel for the truck to pass through. With the cedar roped on like a giant hayrick, the truck nosed into the narrow opening, too narrow by a foot on either side for the Ford to pass through. Dillon, atop the cedar, saw it all unfolding and in a desperate alarm pounded on the roof of the cab, shouting to Olivia, but his voice was lost in the wind. In a swift, rustling sound that felt like a wet, green earthquake, the Ford staggered and stopped in the middle of the bridge, setting off a cacophony of horns from cars piling up behind.

Out front, beyond the soup-can radiator cap, Dillon could see the cars ahead roll silently on over the bridge, leaving an empty expanse of bridge ahead.

Rupert bolted upright, his eyes wide, disheveled hair standing straight up. "What happened? What did you hit?"

"I don't know. It didn't feel like we hit anything."

"Jesus, get out. Get out and see what we hit, will you. We are in the middle of the God damn Second Narrows Bridge." Rupert was shouting again, his voice joining the chorus of automobile horns baying at their heels.

Olivia climbed out into the rain. By the light of the headlights piling up behind the truck she could see Dillon's head sticking out from beneath the tarpaulin. "What happened?" she called out.

"We are stuck," he hollered back.

Olivia studied the load, then leaned back into the cab to face the wild panic in Rupert's eyes. "The load is too wide for the bridge," she said calmly. "We loaded too much on the truck." Olivia was fascinated by the sudden madness of the events while still clinging to the fragile chain of luck that had carried them this far. Rupert fainted carefully across the front seat of the truck, allowing the axe handle tourniquet to spring loose in what swiftly passed through his mind as a suicidal gesture. He was accepting the tragedy of his own dying, preferring to bleed to death rather than face the scene on the bridge.

Olivia climbed back into the cab and began cradling his thin face in her lap and kissing him. The leg had stopped bleeding. "It's okay, baby," she cooed. "Olivia is here and everything is going to be all right. Just you hold on to Ollie, baby." Rupert didn't answer. He was trying to recapture the anonymity of his unconscious state.

Atop the load of cedar, Dillon surveyed what appeared to be a mile or more of headlights backed up behind the truck. Drivers were getting out of their cars and coming in twos and threes to see what was blocking the bridge. Some were pushing aside the side curtains of the Model T to demand Olivia get the truck out of the way.

"Drunk, the bunch of them," said a voice.

"Somebody call the cops," another voice added.

"And look at them kids up there in the rain." Dillon, Isabelle and Louise were all peering out from beneath the tarp. "That guy ought to be in jail. Somebody throw him off the bridge and let's get going."

The threat brought a faint groan from Rupert as the distant cry of a police siren echoed over the water. "My God. Here comes the cops," he muttered and fainted again.

The wail of the siren drowned out the muttering threats surrounding the truck as the police car burst out of the night, coming onto the bridge from the opposite direction, the flashing red light batting at the darkness.

The lone policeman walked over to the truck where Olivia was cradling Rupert's head; he was a grizzled cop of fifty or more, his legs bound in tightly fitted high boots, his chest rising like a pouter pigeon's breast in a tight tunic. The red light had temporarily quieted the honking horns.

"What'n hell is going on?" It wasn't so much a question as it was an indictment as the cop took in the scene; the kids atop the cedar, Rupert unconscious lying across Olivia's lap, and Olivia, her eyes wide with excitement, her baby face alive with animal energy. Yes, he saw Olivia with the same experienced eye that gave him an assessment of the problem.

"He need an ambulance?" Without waiting for an answer he turned and started back to his car. With one foot on the running board he reached through the open window for the radio while looking back at Olivia and the Ford. When he returned to the truck, he was all business, but Olivia sensed a trace of humor that had not been there a moment ago.

"Where's your license, lady?"

"I don't have a license. I never drove before in my life," Olivia answered breathlessly.

"You mean he was driving?"

"Me. I was driving," Olivia tapped her chest proudly. The buttons on her coat had slipped loose and her pointing finger went to the exposed white cleavage of her substantial breasts. "I was trying to get him to a hospital for help."

The policeman scanned the now tilting load of cedar and then looked in at Rupert who was sitting up watching the events unfold. He was trusting Olivia and what she could do with men. He was also concentrating on making the best death mask he could muster in hopes that would somehow extricate him from the scene.

"He that bad?" The policeman sounded skeptical.

"I don't know," Olivia answered. "He cut himself with an axe," she added, aware the cop wasn't looking at Rupert. She made no attempt to close her open coat, aware only of a belly twisting urgency that had been with her since the accident, suspecting the cop was sensing it as well.

"Don't you worry, dolly. He your man?

Olivia shook her head negatively.

"Those kids yours, I suppose?"

Olivia shook her head again. "They are his brothers and sisters."

"I see. Well, everything is going to be just fine. You kids," he hollered up at the load, "stop jumping around up there. There's enough damn confusion without me worrying about you falling off this

bloody bridge." Olivia merely nodded complete
submissiveness to his taking charge.

The car horns started again then, insistently
demanding passage, only to be quickly silenced at
the appearance of the ambulance. Rupert, once again
in a complete collapse, was lifted on a stretcher and
whisked away in the night. Meanwhile, the
policeman moved his car off the bridge, clearing the
way for oncoming traffic; he returned to the truck to
face the backed up traffic. By sheer bluster and
personal presence he began forcing each car back,
an inch at a time, until he had a foot and then two
feet and enough to maneuver. When satisfied, he
came back to Olivia. "Think you can back this thing
up?"

"Sure," she said eagerly. With Rupert taken care
of, she was free to take on the Ford on her own
terms. The policeman didn't miss her mischievous
smile as she hoisted herself into the cab, her coat
having slipped open a notch further. He took the
crank and in a single, powerful spin kicked life into
the engine.

"Now give her hell in reverse," he hollered over
the roar of the Ford's engine. The truck lurched
backward an inch or two and stalled. He cranked
again. "Not so fast this time. Ease into it." Two men
who had drifted up to watch joined him in putting
their shoulders to the truck. Olivia pulled down on
the throttle as the truck struggled ponderously,
disemboweling itself of a large part of the cedar load
as it broke free.

"Whoa. That's far enough," the policeman hollered, joining the others in tossing the strewn evergreens into the Narrows. "Now," he said, smiling up at Olivia, "I want you to take her up on the sidewalk and come forward easy. Got that? Take the two outside wheels onto the sidewalk."

Olivia started the truck forward, the front end mounting the curb followed by the rear wheels, clearing the superstructure by inches. She steered the truck off the bridge and into a pocket beside the road on the opposite side. The grinning policeman, made younger by his victory, produced a notebook from his boot top and stood in the rain waiting for Olivia to step down.

"You want to come to my car. Out of the rain?"

"Sure," she said, and with a parting glance intended to secure the kids in place, followed him into the night. In a short time the police car's headlights went on and the car pulled out into traffic and they were gone. Dillon remained silent, his fragile love shaken. He had seen Olivia like that before.

"Do you think she's been arrested?" Isabelle was imagining the worst. Dillon wished that she had. "She doesn't have a driver's license, does she," Isabelle added, confirming her own fears. "And this truck doesn't belong to Rupert, does it."

"And it has only one headlight," her sister Louise added in an equally fatal voice as they huddled together in the bed of cedar boughs.

After what seemed hours, though it was something less than an hour, the police car reappeared. From the truck, the kids couldn't see Olivia getting out but she appeared suddenly alongside the truck, materializing out of the darkness, her face flushed and smiling. She climbed back into the cab with an air of confidence, adjusted the hand spark and throttle and stepped outside to crank the engine. "Dillon, climb down out of there and shut the throttle down when she starts," she called up to Dillon. He took the seat behind the wheel as Olivia leaned over the engine cowling as if she had been cranking automobiles all her life. Quickly, easily, she spun the engine to life.

"Now," she announced, easing Dillon from behind the wheel, "we are going to get this truck home." Olivia turned the truck into the traffic, trusting to something other than the single headlight as she steered into the string of passing cars. Passing the spot where they had pulled off the road, the police car's headlights blinked on and off. Dillon knew they were speaking to Olivia.

Meanwhile, the ambulance had taken Rupert to the emergency ward of St. Paul's Hospital, where the cut on his leg required eight stitches and a large swath of tape and bandage. He was dismissed with no charge and rode the tram home. He appeared dramatically at the kitchen door, using one hand to steady his gait and walking with a magnificent limp. He paused a long moment in the kitchen light, giving the entire house a chance to take in his gray face and bloodied trousers before entering with news of the truck and his leg wound.

"The kids are okay," he said in response to Molly Costello's panic. "I would never have allowed them to take me away if I hadn't been sure that everything was under control. There's dozens of men taking care of things. I was assured the Provincial Police will see they all get home safely. It was the police who made me leave," he added.

When the Ford rumbled into the Costello yard, Rupert, who had said he needed to lie down, was immediately at the kitchen door as the last of the kids bailed down from the cedar load. Rupert's brothers, aware the truck had been 'borrowed', were already unloading the cedar in their rush to get the truck back to the junkyard.

Olivia ignored them all, marching the kids into the house as if she was leading a victorious scout troop. When they were all accounted for, she released a great sigh. "There. We bloody well made it, kids." She wore a satisfied grin on her face as she dropped into a chair by the stove.

"Your dinner is in the warming oven," Molly said, attempting to conceal her relief at the sight of her kids in one piece. She was not about to ask for the story from Olivia, yet she couldn't conceal the good feeling that swelled up around this woman who had delivered her children from the night. "You drove them home. In that truck," she said softly. Then without waiting for an answer, "Let me get your supper for you."

Rupert stood out of Molly's line of sight, mouthing a message to Olivia to play it cool and say nothing. Olivia smiled mysteriously at him and dug into her jacket to produce a package of expensive Craven A cigarettes. She then leaned over the stove, tipped the lid to expose the flames, and with her long, damp hair almost in the fire puffed the cigarette to life. She then blew a superbly confident, long, straight cloud of smoke across the table, smiling her thanks to Molly.

"I have eaten, but the kids must be starved," she announced.

"Eaten? Where," Rupert demanded, having spotted the expensive cigarettes.

"The policeman. You remember? The one who helped us off the bridge. He bought me a burger. Said I was a swell driver, too," Olivia answered, unable to suppress the tease from her voice.

"That fat old bugger? What did he want?" Rupert was no longer playing it cool for Molly. His instinct and knowledge of his woman had set flames loose in his head. "That old cop wouldn't buy his own mother a hamburger."

"Not many of you would," Molly said, turning on him.

"Well, I'm not exactly his mother," Olivia added, pulling deliciously on her cigarette.

Late into the night Dillon could hear their voices coming through the wall, muffled and tense at first, and then interspersed with periods of silence. Finally there came the soft sounds of Olivia's laughter, followed by the rhythmic noises he had heard during each night of their stay.

###

Pappas' Pants

The people were Greek and they spoke very simple English.

"You been fighting," Mrs. Pappas said.

Angelo nodded. Yes, he had been fighting.

"You ripped your shirt and your nose is bleeding," Mrs. Pappas said.

Angelo nodded again and rubbed the back of his hand across his lip where the blood had dried. A small trickle started again out of his nose. The shirt was beyond help.

"Why you fight?" Mrs. Pappas said. "Why you fight and rip your shirt and get your nose bleeding."

"Because of my pants," Angelo said. He looked proud, like he had been fighting for his country.

"What's the matter with you pants?" his momma said.

"Nothing is the matter," Angelo said. He pulled at the top of his trousers so that the crotch came up to his knees and the green woolen cuffs rose imperceptibly above his shoe tops.

"You nose is bleeding again," Mrs. Pappas said. "Somebody didn't like you pants?"

"Yes," Angelo said. "They are the cause of all of my fighting. There is nothing good in these pants except the pocket in the back that has no hole in it."

"Your poppa wore those pants and he never fought in them like you do," Mrs. Pappas said.

"That's because he had tuberculosis," Angelo said. "Nobody would fight him because he was sick.

Besides, the pants were better when poppa wore them."

"Who did you fight over the pants?" Mrs. Pappas said.

"The Irish boys," Angelo said.

"You mean the Murphy boys?"

"The Murphy boys and the others," Angelo said.

"What do the Murphy boys says about your pants to make you fight with them?" Mrs. Pappas said.

"They call them Pappas Poppa's Pants." Angelo ducked his head, ready for a cuff on the ear. But his momma had only reached out to put a hand on his head.

"Your poppa was proud of those pants. He wore those pants to church. You should be proud to wear his pants," Mrs. Pappas said.

"Yes," Angelo said.

"When your poppa went to work in those pants he always did good things. I saved those pants for you because you are his son. I want you to be like your poppa. You should wear his pants," she said. She was from the old country.

"But I am not going to work. I am going to school. And it is hard to run in these pants. If I had a pair of pants of my own I could run and the Irish wouldn't trip me and pretend it was the pants that tripped me. I wouldn't fight if I had my own pants."

Mrs. Pappas looked at him for a long time. She was thinking. "Do you want an apple?" she said. "You wash and I'll give you an apple. And Angelo, you wear your poppa's pants for a little while longer.

If you have to fight, it's good you fight for your poppa's pants."

###

The Champion

Dado Marino was the world flyweight champion, or maybe he was the world bantamweight champion, I'm not certain, it was so long ago and we had so many titles floating around in those days. It is enough to say he was so tiny that a mother would want to take him up in her arms; he was a mere wisp of a man from the Philippines with a calm and innocent face. He was working out in the Georgia Arena and when we saw him, he was standing in one corner of the ring wearing soft cotton trousers and a loose sweatshirt, punching silently at an invisible opponent.

"Which one of you wants to go a round with the champeen of the world?" The man making the offer was a thick-set, sweating Chinese who talked with a New York accent. He was waving a towel at the champion, keeping time with the silent blows being rained on the invisible opponent. But there was something in the tempting way the invitation was being offered that said, "Be careful." The Chinaman's nose was melded into his face and his ears had taken on enough retreads that they had the look of flowering mushrooms sprouting beneath his thick, black hair.

"The champeen needs the work, fellas. He's lookin' to exercise. Won't hit you. You just get in the ring and try hitting him. Who's game?" The offer was difficult to refuse, the champion being so small and all.

It was a Thursday morning, two days before the fight. The unemployed and the uneducated and the uninvolved among us had come down to the old arena to watch the workout. None of us moved until someone shoved Jake McGregor from behind. "How about Jake?"

"Naw. I'm too big," Jake protested. Even in his teens, he was better than two hundred pounds. Jake the Moose, we called him.

"You are just right," said the Chinese. He pulled the ropes apart and looked down at Jake's tennis shoes. "You even got the right shoes." We laughed and joked Jake through the ropes and watched while he clowned around imitating the champion's shadow boxing routine. The Chinese began lacing big, red leather gloves over his fists and Jake was making faces at the rest of us when the tiny Philippine fighter came out of his corner toward him.

It was a biblical scene, Jake six feet and big all over and Dado Marino, no bigger than a modest twelve-year-old. Whoosh, Jake took a solid shot with his right that would have lifted the little man out of the ring. The champion bent easily from the waist and the shot went high. Whoosh, whoosh, this time the punches came lower but seemed to slip harmlessly off the little man's arms. Then, with no effort at all, Dado Marino stepped inside Jake's arms and began whopping his gloves into the kidney and midsection, the punches sounding like bullets going into a wet mattress.

Whoosh, whoosh, Jake fired off a few more and the little fellow shot out a left hook that crashed into

the side of Jake's head and knocked him on his can.
There wasn't much left of old Jake after that and the
Chinese was already unlacing the gloves by the time
Jake looked out through the ropes and shook his
head.

"Who's next? Nobody gets hurt and you can go
home and tell your folks how you boxed with the
champeen. Come on," the Chinaman urged as he
helped ease Jake over the ring apron. Danny
Sweeney climbed into the ring.

Now so far as any of us knew, Danny never
fought anyone in his life, at least not so's you would
call it a fight. But Danny was as Irish as the freckles
on his face and the fire in his red hair and when
pressed, why he would dance a fancy circle around
you, fists flashing menacingly in the air until you
were winded just watching him go by. As far as
fighting goes, Danny was a dancing man. The
Chinaman looked him over warily.

"You ever fight, kid?" It was as if he had spotted
something in the way Danny stepped into the ring
that made him pause. We could have told him not to
worry. Danny would dance his way out of a fight
every time, even when he was mixing it up with
Hughie Forbes, who got whipped once a week by
his kid sister.

"Tell him not to hit me hard," Danny said as the
Chinaman laced on the gloves. Danny and the
champion were almost the same weight, though
Danny was a head taller and with his shirt off you
could see how solid he was through the shoulders.

The Chinaman muttered a few words to the champion and he came out slowly. Danny began moving in a circle to his right. He was a southpaw and he put out his right hand pawing at the air, sketching an outline of the champion who threw a quick combination that caught Danny on the arms. Then the Philippine man bent at the waist and came in under Danny's pawing right hand and banged home two solid punches to the belly that sent Danny backing toward the ropes. But just as he stepped back out of reach, Danny let go the left and it caught the champion flush between the eyes, snapping his head back.

"Easy, kid." The shout came from the Chinese corner man. We hoped he was hollering at the champion. Some of us wanted to cheer for Danny but we were afraid for his life after he had hit the little man. That's when Danny began shuffling. In and out. Quick stepping one foot forward then back, moving with that back foot set flat behind him with each step like he did on the street. And here was the champion following him, cautiously feinting, in and out, throwing a left and missing and another that glanced off the head. Danny looked like he had been doing this all his life.

The champion caught him in the midsection again and then followed up with an overhand looping right that smacked into Danny's ear. Even as the punch landed, wham, Danny's left came crashing into the chest, sending the champion staggering back across the ring.

When the Chinaman climbed back into the ring, Danny was still standing, a big red welt showing around his waist and a blue bruise rising below his right eye. But he was still slapping those long-arm punches at the champion, who was carrying a couple of heavy red welts of his own. "That's enough. Time," shouted the Chinaman. Dado Marino laced his arms around Danny's middle and escorted him to our side of the ring.

"You pretty good, kid," he said. "You hit hard. Too hard." And he grinned and rubbed his face with the back of his glove. "You could be good, kid. Cyrus," he said to the Chinese, "you got a place on the card for this kid?"

Danny shook his head. He was in a hurry to shed the gloves. "I'm a dancer, not a fighter," he mumbled through a swollen lip. And they shook hands. Just the same, none of us gave Danny the invitation to 'put 'em up' ever again.

###

Licentious Thoughts

He hadn't noticed her arrival. Stretched out in the early September sunshine, his mind was somewhere in that haze between dozing and dreaming, the world around him in some distant universe. But she was upwind and the scent, her perfume or sun lotion, sweet and soft on the warm air, opened his eyes.

When she realized he was watching her she smiled. "Hi."

" Hi," he answered, turning over on his belly to study her in earnest. She was long legged and sun brown, wearing a thin halter over what the underwear ads would call extra-full breasts. The a snug, hip-hugging set of shorts she wore rose up to expose soft, white flesh where her rump came down to cup the top of her thighs.

Somewhere from the basement of his mind came an echo of the soft Georgia accent of Jimmy Carter confessing to having lusted in his mind. He had never met Jimmy Carter but he could hear him just the same, baring his conscience to the editors of Playboy Magazine with his confession to having lusted in his thoughts.

She raised herself on one elbow so that he thought she was about to drop out of the halter, and once again he heard the softly modulated words of the President of the United States: "Now in my mind I have lusted after women other than my wife. I have committed adultery many times lusting and all that. In my mind." Even the Georgia penitent couldn't utter that last definitive word.

She smiled, turning halfway toward the door to examine her reflection in the glass guarding the edge of the pool deck from the wind. Then rising on her haunches, her hands above her head, elbows extended, she adjusted her hair. "Everyone should be forgiving of the transgression of others. Men who are faithful to their wives should not judge the men who would screw a lot of women," Jimmy had said, or something close to those words. She reached across the expanse between the deck chairs and picked up the book he had been reading.

"Poet? What a funny name for a book. What's it about?"

"It's about an Irishman who couldn't decide what he wanted in women."

"What happened to him?"

"He married one and fell in love with another. In the end he left them both for a beautiful stranger."

"You finished the book already?"

" I wrote it."

"You read your own books? I would think..."

"I'm working on a screenplay from the book," he lied.

"For the movies?"

"Why? You want to be in the movies," he laughed.

"Oh sure. Me and my three kids."

"Which are yours?"

She pointed to the pool. "That one with her butt out of the water and the two boys trying to drown one another at the other end."

The fires of lust began rapidly dimming. It was easier to corral ones thoughts when thinking about a mother of three kids. Even if she did have that great-looking body. She could see the change in his eyes. "I take it you don't like kids."

"Depends. I have a couple of my own. Sometimes they are downright decent. Sometimes I wish I didn't know them."

She shook her head and rose up off the lounge chair as if the news of his family had closed the book on him as well.

"Would you keep an eye on mine for me for a minute? I have to make a phone call."

"An eye? You want me to keep an eye on them? If keeping an eye doesn't mean my jumping in the water or anything dramatic, okay?"

"Thanks. I'll be right back," she said and left, carrying his book.

He had just closed his eyes when a sprinkle of pool water brought his head back up.

"Where did my mom go?" The long legged, skinny girl stood with her arms stretched out like a scarecrow, shaking the water from her body over his legs. He wondered if genetic evolution would some day bless her with the sensational ass he had just watched disappear through the swinging doors.

"To make a phone call," he said, hoping his indifferent tone would convince the kid of his complete lack of accountability.

"Are you supposed to be watching us?"

"What is it you want me to watch?"

"My dad watches me swim underwater."

"I'll bet."

"I scare him. He doesn't know how long I can hold my breath. Watch." She jumped back into the pool.

The offer made him nervous. "I would rather you didn't. Save it for your dad."

"I don't have a dad anymore," the skinny girl said and pinched her nose between her thumb and forefinger and went under the water.

"Wait." But she had submerged. He could see her long skinny body porpoise out from the wall, the green ripples on the surface adding kinks and curves to her legs. He got up and walked to the edge of the pool. "Damn," he muttered and started alongside the pool, tracking her as she headed into the deeper water.

"Where's Ellen?" The mother's voice at his ear spun him around.

"That's her playing Admiral Rickover in the deep end. She says she has great staying power under water, you know what I mean?"

As he spoke he noticed the kid had stopped kicking and her arms were no longer pulling her through the water. "She's stopped," he said quietly.

"Ellen. That's enough," the mother shouted across the surface of the pool but the kid's body just turned slowly face up beneath the surface.

"SHIT," he heard himself shout as he hit the surface of the pool. He was still going down as the kid broke the surface. When he came up for air, the kid was laughing.

" I told ya," the kid hollered between catching her breath. "I scared you too, didn't I."

The mother was holding his book. "I looked at this. You really did write it. Your picture is on the cover. You know, I am an actress. I have been in lots of plays. Were you serious about..." She never finished.

"Forget it," he said, pulling himself onto the pool deck. "I was lying about the screenplay."

###

Taxes

"What did you do with all those doctor bills?"

"What doctor bills?"

"Those bills that have been coming in here all year long. We have been getting more mail from doctors than a lonely hearts club and you ask, 'What bills?' The kid's sore foot. Your backache. My heart murmurings. Those bills."

"You never said you wanted me to keep those bills."

"Listen. I'm doing our income tax returns. They sent us the blank income tax forms in the mail today and I'm doing them myself this year. Why not? The government says any idiot can do them. I need all those bills for deductions from our taxable income. It's that simple."

" Good luck." She shrugs like it's only me that's going to jail.

"And I'm gonna need our telephone bills. I think we can deduct the taxes we pay on all our long distance telephone calls too."

"Long distance calls?"

"Don't be smart. And how about the interest payments on the car? How much interest did we pay on the car anyway? On the house? On the credit cards? Boy, by the time I get through with this, the government is going to owe us real money."

"Where do you think you are going to get all that stuff?"

"Never mind making it tough. It's tough enough already. We gotta get to work right now and get our refund. How about depreciation? Let's figure out what we can claim in depreciation. Everybody is claiming depreciation."

"What's to depreciate?" I can see she's trying, but not yet into the swing of it.

"Well, we depreciate anything that gets old and wears out. Anything that isn't worth what it was worth when we bought it. That's what depreciation is all about."

You could tell by her face that she had heard something in that which was not intended. "Look. If we are going to get into personalities, you are not holding up like any Paul Newman yourself, kiddo," she replied.

"It's not people. You only depreciate people when they are professionals, hockey players or baseball players. That's how come they pay so much to sign those basketball players. A million-dollars-a-year player with a five-year contract, that's all part of some millionaire's write off. That's why they say those pro ball clubs don't make any money. It's all depreciation."

"We don't have any pro ball players. Just Ella. She helps me with the bathrooms on Mondays. She's just about out on her feet. Maybe we could...." She let the idea die on it's own.

"Forget it. But we do have dependents. There's the kids, that's three. Then there's you." Another dirty look.

"Whose side are you on, anyway? You are a dependent. Then there's your mother? Lots of guys declare their mother-in-law."

"I'll bet most of 'em are still living."

"Well, skip your mother. Let's get going. Line one. That's easy. Write down your name. And while we are at it, how about all the local taxes we pay and our drivers' licenses and the dog license? Damn. The pencil broke. What do you mean I can't do this in pencil? Who says you are not going to sign it? Nobody goes to jail if they give honest answers. Mistakes don't count."

She shakes her head and walks out of the room but remains in hollering range, and I call after her.

"What would you rather have me do? Use that short form for idiots? Pay through the nose like we did all those other years? Listen. If we do this right, we will get a big rebate. All those people with accountants get rebates. Those places that fill out your tax form for a fee will even lend you the rebate in advance."

No answer.

"Okay then. I'll use the short form and we will probably die broke."

###

Henry Calder

Henry Calder awoke to the sound of the horse-drawn milk wagon rumbling past the house, the heavy four-wheel wagon moving at a pace that allowed the milkman to sprint up to each succeeding door without the wagon ever coming to a full stop. Henry lay motionless, listening to the clink of the glass bottles nudging one another on the milkman's trot to the porch. Carefully, expectantly, he opened his eyes to the daylight invading the bedroom through the tan blinds drawn full shade to hold back the morning.

He felt the oppressive presence of Laura Jean's body pressing against his side and shifted in the bed, searching for a fresh spot in the sheets. He failed; stretching his legs, his thoughts turned to the coming day. It was the first day of Hudson's School's summer vacation, Henry's day of liberation from the classroom of impudent, cunning, sixth-graders, to be free of his role as a paragon of physical and intellectual perfection. Checking out of school for the summer was an opportunity to escape his highly structured life into the absolute anonymity of a summer job. It was a transition allowing Henry to shuck the character molded from boyhood by his father, who read Kipling and had reared his son as he would an English public school boy, with caning as a matter of principle administered once a week, along with a constant monitoring of his academic progress.

Henry knew that within a half hour of rising, he would step into a life of a man of his own making, a person conceived in boyhood fantasies. It didn't matter that he would return home each night to step back into the life of the Henry Calder his father knew. That Henry, his father's Henry, the husband of Laura Jean, would retreat from the romantic, dark-haired buccaneer of his summer life.

This was the day Henry was to report for war work in the North Burrard Shipyards. He had applied for the job and trained as a lead riveter with the same secretiveness he maintained when he took up mowing the summer grass at the Jericho Golf and Country Club; or the summer spent in a packing plant canning beans and peaches. None of those careers were discussed with his father, nor Laura Jean. It was only as the summers unfolded that the character he shaped around each new job emerged in a line of casual conversation, a telltale pay slip, a check stub or a ferry ticket. There would come a day each summer when it would be as if they had known all along what he was doing, but never as a result of his explaining nor consulting them.

Henry's formula for a successful marriage decreed that a man was not accountable to his wife. Laura Jean accepted this, just as she accepted the summer personality he created around his new work, confident that come fall, Henry, her Henry, would return as her university-educated husband. It was Henry's father, a widower the year his son turned five, who had selected Laura Jean from a convention of elementary school teachers to become Henry's wife. She was two years older than his son, a steadying influence, the elder Calder reasoned, as if measuring the heft of a dray horse. His choosing Laura Jean also served to extend the elder Calder's authority to Henry's house, where the old man's appearance sent the bride into subservient obsequiousness.

Both Henry and his father regarded Laura Jean as an appendage to his career, originally targeted toward a degree in anthropology. Henry's boyhood dreams were once filled with visions of professional athletics. His height, five feet five inches, ruled that out, though not before he had exercised his chest and arm muscles until he took on the appearance of an inverted bowling pin. It was the Great Depression that redirected his career to the public schools and a fourth-through-seventh-grades assignment teaching physical education and math.

Reporting to the shipyard as a lead hand, he wore a tight fitting suit of bib coveralls over a turtleneck sweater that exposed the muscles of his upper torso. Damp sweat stains shading the armpits added to the man of steel image he was striving for. It was an appearance that gave a swagger to his walk as he came across the open deck toward his crew, his hard hat tilted back on his head, his black curls falling carelessly over his forehead.

"Hiya. I'm Hank, Hank Calder." Henry had dropped all trace of his 'educated' classroom manner, sounding more Texan than teacher. He extended a hand to the wiry dwarf of a man standing between the two teenaged boys who made up the rivet crew. "They tell me I'm your new lead man." The little man accepted the handshake in a hard, dry fist.

"Can't believe it," the little man muttered, his words escaping through teeth clenched on a cigarette.

"Can't? Can't believe what?"

The little man, his eyes concealed beneath the brim of a large hard hat that came down over his ears, shook his head sadly. "Gather this is your first job in the yard?" His eyes went to Henry's soft hands, his leather apron and boots, untouched by the hot steel that burned its mark on those who worked the plates.

"Yep," Henry replied. "But keep in mind; I was the number one trainee in the yard riveting school. So you don't need to worry about me."

"Don't mean shit to me, mister. We get paid piece work on hull jobs, so we'll try and keep you from catching a hot rivet up your ass." Two boys, members of the crew, laughed. "Name's Carmody," the little man added. "I'm your bucker." Henry felt his face tighten as he struggled to mask a surge of irritation.

"We all here?" he asked briskly. "Passer. Cooker. You're the bucker. Where's the other passer? One passer is missing." The warning shift whistle shrieked over the yard and Carmody shrugged, shouting over the blast.

"A dame. Our second passer's a dame. Who in hell knows about dames."

"To hell with it. Let's get started without her," Henry barked over the rising din of the awakening yard. He began to uncoil the pressure hose to his gun when he caught sight of a woman's head and shoulders coming up through the deck opening. She swung off the ladder, her cheeks puffed in pantomime as she gasped for air.

"What a helluva climb." The girl pretended to stagger across the deck, her large, soft, brown eyes measuring Henry as she came. "Hi. I'm Mary Lou. You're the new rivet banger. Right?"

"Right," Henry stammered.

"Then thank God I'm in the right place. I don't think I could make it up another ladder. Hey. Look who's here. Carmody. We go again, eh, old timer?"

Carmody offered the girl a sly grin. "Never mind that old timer shit." Then to Henry, "Watch your step with this one. She can be a real hair up your ass."

"Sez who, you old fart? Gimme a drag." Mary Lou plucked the cigarette out of the little man's mouth, drew deeply enough to make the end burn brightly, and then blew the smoke in his face. "Okay. I'm winded but I'm ready," she said, turning her smile on Henry.

Eight ten-thousand ton Victory Ship hulls lay in a row like disemboweled whales beached in the summer sun, their sterns suspended above the water of the inner harbor, webs of tangled compressor hose and electric welding lines twitching and hissing in and out of their innards. The second shift whistle died out, the sound of the yard coming to life rising over the hulls, growing louder and louder until it filled the air with the industrial roar of the war.

"Been here long?" Mary Lou shouted above the chatter of the compressor.

"First day," Henry shouted, stepping back from the bulkhead in response to her smile. They stood gazing at one another until Carmody's face appeared from behind the plate. He was braced against the steel, awaiting the first rivet.

"What the hell," he yelled. "We going to drive rivets or are you two going to make eyes at each other all day?" Mary Lou gave Henry an exasperated shrug and signaled for a rivet. It came soaring through the air, a red-hot steel missile that she snatched in flight. In one flowing motion, she pinched the burning slug between long handled tongs and plugged it in the steel plate so close to Henry's face the heat seemed to scorch his cheek.

"Old bugger is jealous," Mary Lou shouted. "Carmody's got the hots for every girl in the yard." Her words were lost in the din of steel hammering on steel. Henry was unable to hear the sound of her voice again until the lunch whistle quieted the yard. Mary Lou dropped her gloves onto the deck and propped her fists on her hips. "What are we supposed to call you?"

"Hank's just fine." Mary Lou raised an eyebrow quizzically.

"Hank Calder," Henry assured her. "What do I call you?"

"My last name is kinda mixed up, if you know what I mean," she explained. "Used to be one thing then I got mixed up with a couple of guys and it changed. Call me Mary Lou for now, eh?" she said making a nest of their coats next to the bulkhead. "Sit down, Hank. This isn't a bed," she grinned. "I'm not that dangerous. Around here, I get called everything from Dumplings to Dolly, but don't you start. You call me Mary Lou and I'll call you Hank, though you sure as hell don't look like a Hank to me."

He hesitated and she looked up with a laugh. "This isn't a bed."

Henry sat next to her and began making an engineering project out of peeling an orange. Mary Lou rummaged through his lunch pail, talking as she explored his sandwiches. "I been here eight months. Some people think it's a bad idea for a woman to do this kind of work, eh. Hell, in the yard I make more in a week than I made in a month in Spencer's housewares. Ever go shopping at Spencer's, Hank? Uh-uh. I guess not," she said.

Henry was attempting to maintain a conversation when she reached across his lap for her own lunch pail, his entire body stiffening at the touch of her thigh against his leg. "I guess it can be rough around here, for a girl?" He stammered, his classroom voice creeping back into his words. He was picturing her lined up at the row of single-cell portable toilets where a single sheet of corrugated metal separated the 'women's' shed from the long line of open urinals. She read his mind.

"You mean, with all these men around, Hank? Things are only rough for a girl when there are no

men around. You won't ever hear a gal complain
when there are too many men. Hell, the only time
anybody notices a woman in the yard is when we
line up for the can." She had taken half his orange
and spoke through the juice running down her chin.
"Most guys around here are kids or old men like
Carmody, who's got a hard-on half the time. But
he's no different from the rest. I can handle the likes
of him. I don't know what I'll do if this war ever
ends."

The warning whistle brought her to her feet. She
reached over and lifted Henry's hard hat from his
head, peered inside the safety webbing, then pointed
a finger in his face with mock authority.

"Hank Calder. I have to get this thing decorated
to yard standards. Be back in two shakes of a lamb's
tail, honey." Henry grabbed playfully at the hat but
she jumped beyond his reach and started down the
steel ladder. The second work whistle sounded,
bringing the air compressors to life with a roar.
Henry fired his rivet gun against the steel bulkhead,
signaling the crew. One of the teenagers picked up
Mary Lou's bucket and the work went on without
her.

It was a half hour later when he turned at the
sound of her voice close to his ear. Mary Lou had
come up behind him. "You are going to catch one
of those rivets in the ear without a helmet," she said,
panting for breath. Carmody shouted something
over the roar of the compressor and Mary Lou shot
back. "Up yours, old man. Keep that up and I'm

going to cut you off." Carmody laughed and the crew fell back into the rhythm of the afternoon.

"Your helmet is over by your bucket," she shouted at Henry. "Leave it in the sun until the paint dries." Henry glanced over his shoulder. His helmet, white in the yard identification for lead hands, now bore blue letters across the brow spelling out "Hank."

Henry and Mary Lou ate together each day of that first week in July, nesting in the shade of a bulkhead out of the sun, where Mary Lou's playful intimacy raised the temperature for Henry in a way that excited and frustrated him. Each day her laughter ended with the sound of the shift whistle, which signaled her return to the roll of a disinterested co-worker. That is, until Friday of Henry's second week in the yard, his first pay day. He wasn't aware of her standing behind him in the line to the pay window until she yanked his shirttail out of the back of his trousers.

"Hey, Hank, baby. What are ya going to do with all that money? You know it's a rule around here that the lead hand gets to buy the first round on payday. You're comin' up to the Lonsdale Arms with us, right? Going to show us how much you appreciate our war effort? You are doing this for the war effort, aren't you, Hank? I mean, you aren't just doing this to keep out of the army, eh?" She laughed and jerked loose the rest of his shirttail. Henry blushed, unable to parry her laughter.

"Why not?" he said uncertainly. "Let's go."

As they passed through the yard gates, the afternoon sun had begun to settle beyond the harbor, leaving the first breath of an evening breeze gusting gently up Lower Lonsdale Avenue in the wake of the day. The air and Mary Lou's arm laced through his own lifted the fatigue from Henry's shoulders as she steered him through the leaded glass doors into the 'Ladies Section' of the North Shore Arms; this portion of the 'Licensed Premises' was reserved by law for women drinkers and male escorts. Mary Lou spotted Carmody and the two teenagers from the crew drinking in the 'Men's Section' and waved to Carmody.

"Send us over a couple of beers," Carmody hollered. "Charge them to Hank and we will leave you two alone." He grinned woefully at the two boys and they all laughed.

During the next two hours, nurtured on the flow of beer and the suggestive warmth of Mary Lou's thigh pressed against his leg beneath the table, Henry's shipyard character emerged, fully formed. When he finally sailed out of the beer parlor into the warm summer evening, the beer buzzing in his head, Henry had his arm wrapped possessively around her waist. He stopped in the middle of Lonsdale Avenue, pulled her to him and kissed her on the mouth, his hand sliding down her back to rest on her behind. Mary Lou merely smiled expectantly.

They boarded the eight o'clock ferry at the foot of Lonsdale along with two uniformed B.C. Electric Streetcar workers and a handful of girls in white shipyard coveralls coming off an overtime shift.

Henry maneuvered Mary Lou against the stern railing of the empty car deck, holding her there with his body while his hand went groping deep into her coverall pockets for her cigarettes. He came up with the pack and placed a cigarette between her lips. Recalling a scene from a John Garfield movie, he lit his own cigarette then touched the burning end to Mary Lou's. The kiss that followed tasted of beer and tobacco and lingered soft and wet on his mouth.

Henry made no attempt to shed his shipyard character when he swaggered through the front door, one of Mary Lou's cigarettes dangling from his lip. It was as if he was purposefully flaunting his new image the minute he entered the house. It was quarter past ten and Laura Jean, her face creamed for bed, her hair twisted in tight metal curlers, sat wrapped in her dressing gown reading beneath a desk lamp.

"You are late," she observed more out of curiosity than asking for an explanation. Henry tapped his cigarette ash into the cuff of his coveralls, inhaled deeply, and shot a stream of smoke across the room as he dropped heavily into the easy leather chair. Laura Jean sniffed the cloud of cigarette smoke distastefully. Before she could begin to question the appearance of this new character, the telephone began ringing. Ignoring the phone, she managed to get off her first question

"Henry? That's a cigarette you are smoking?"

He extended his cigarette between two fingers at arm's length with mock astonishment.

"Why, yea. So it seems."

"But we have always considered cigarettes rather vulgar."

"You and my father have considered them vulgar. Is that what you are saying? I rather enjoy them. Relaxing. Refreshing. How about you? Like one?" He held out Mary Lou's package of Player's Mild. When she appeared unable to understand, he dismissed the subject with: "Answer the phone."

"Please, Henry." she muttered. "A good pipe is more your style. As an academician, it's more in keeping for you to smoke a pipe." She was about to mention the strong odor of beer that had followed him into the house, thought better of it and picked up the phone.

Henry smiled, satisfied at the revulsion on her face.

"It's your father, Henry." Laura Jean held out the telephone with a look on her face implying he was about to face his day of reckoning. Henry's chin dropped to his chest and he closed his eyes as if he had suddenly slipped off into a doze.

"Just a minute, Father. He's right here, sitting in your chair, as well. Henry, I said it's your father." Henry blinked blankly, accepting the phone reluctantly.

"Henry?" The sound of his father's voice seemed to overcome him with a great weariness. He felt very tired.

"Yesss."

"What is the matter, son? You don't sound too chipper?" A long silence. "Henry? You there?"

"Yesss. I'm here."

"Well pay attention, son. I called to tell you the committee has decided to ask you to take over as director of Christ Church Sunday School's junior program beginning in September. Henry? That means you will be in charge of the entire lower school. Did you hear me?"

"Yesss." His father's enthusiasm failed to extricate Henry from the warm memory of Mary Lou's soft body.

"The dean himself called this evening. He personally chose you. He told me the committee had considered that Smithson chap, the mathematics man from General Gordon School? They though him a trifle swift and I couldn't agree more. I mean, look at the clothes he wears. We have always dressed you in a sensible, academic vein, and it has paid off. Paid off indeed, eh?" The elder Calder's words filtered ponderously through Henry's beer fogged mind. "Henry? What do you say, son?"

"I'm thinking, Father."

"Thinking? Good Lord, Henry, thinking about what? There's fifty-five a month that goes with the post. You know what that would mean to the car fund, son."

There it was, a paramount reason for Henry's summer job, the only reason the old man had put up with his son's summer fantasies for the past three years. Since buying their house with Laura Jean's inheritance, every spare dime had been dedicated to the purchase of a car. Laura Jean's hysterectomy took nearly three hundred from the fund. That put the purchase back a year. Then the elder Calder needed two hundred for new teeth. Still, the fund was closing in on eight hundred dollars, the total printed precisely in the pages of the family savings book. The three of them had spent each Sunday in the last month of June visiting automobile showrooms.

"It means one or two mid-week meetings with the liturgical committee and some coordinating time with the dean. But we don't want to be turning up our noses on fifty-five a month, Henry. Not at all." Henry was trying to picture Mary Lou's reaction to his telling her he had been appointed superintendent of a Sunday school.

"Fifty-five a month isn't enough," Henry said quietly and set the telephone receiver back on the hook. He adjusted himself in the easy chair and lit a second cigarette. Laura Jean had gone to bed and before the telephone began ringing again, he buried the receiver in a pile of cushions, closed his eyes and went once more in search of Mary Lou.

∗∗∗

The following day, Henry's crew was on piecework, setting deck plates in the ship's mid-section, driving hard through the heat of the morning when the compressor line went limp. Henry was stripped to the waist, sweat glistening on the hairs of his chest and forming rivulets over his flat belly. "God damn. What's the bloody trouble now?" He slammed the impotent rivet gun to the deck and sucked in a deep breath. Mary Lou pulled the cotton wool from her ears.

"What's that?" She had removed her underclothes during the mid-morning break and her heavy coveralls hung loosely from her body, her sweat showing in shadowy stains beneath her arms and down her back, outlining her body's full, soft curves beneath.

"Pressure's gone," Henry said and kicked the rivet gun across the deck. He reached for his wristwatch in the pocket of his coveralls. "I'll go see what's happened. You might as well get out of the sun." When he reappeared the others were gone, leaving only Mary Lou on the deck.

"Carmody took the kids below into the shade," she explained. "What's up?"

"Maintenance disconnected us to feed a crew on a lower deck that's behind schedule. They say we will be down an hour or more." Henry removed his helmet and swiped a sleeve across his brow. "How about a Coke?"

"Anything to get out of this sun."

Henry followed her down the steel ladders into the warm shadows below the steel deck. Mary Lou wiggled through a hatch in the bulkhead and into the ballast tanks near the propeller shaft. A string of temporary light bulbs ran as far as the hatch opening, leaving the interior dark. Mary Lou turned and looked back at him with an unspoken invitation and led the way into the dark. She laughed teasingly as he came up behind her, slipped his arm around her waist and began fumbling with the buttons on her coveralls. His hand pushed aside the buttons to reveal her breast. In that instant he was struck with a vision of Laura Jean. The picture flashed before him as clearly as if she had stepped through the steel bulkhead. She wore her shapeless nightgown and was frowning in mute denunciation.

That same vision had appeared to him once before. It happened during the Hudson School teachers' Christmas party when Henry kissed Alicia Henderson, the third grade music teacher, in the teacher's lounge. Impulsively he had pushed his hand down the front of Miss Henderson's skirt into her underpants. Alicia Henderson was receptive enough, but at that moment Laura Jean had materialized as clearly as if she were standing in the room. Henry had frozen with the lavender-smelling Alicia Henderson's rump in his hands, his eyes fixed on the image of Laura Jean. He could see the hairs on her lip curl up as she sneered indignantly. Alicia Henderson's breath was blasting in his face like a dog in summer heat but the vision had been enough for Henry to immediately jerk his hand free of her groin.

Mary Lou put her mouth on his, thrusting her tongue between his lips like a reptile in search of a den. Henry felt her warm body against his, inhaled the scent of her sweat as the cacophony of steel shipbuilding flooded his brain, annihilating all thought of Laura Jean. Mary Lou reached up and pulled his head to her large breasts and together they slowly collapsed onto the steel bulkhead in the ethereal darkness.

In the days that followed Henry became a game for Mary Lou. She delighted in leading him into a world where she was a thousand years wiser, playing him as if he were an undisciplined pet and laughing at his adolescent love making. He was unable to keep from touching her, brushing against her, squeezing her arm, constantly reaching out to come in contact with her body. She began to push him away, tolerantly, at first with frowns that turned to slapping until, petulantly, she would openly turn on him in front of the crew.

"Damn it, Hank, find yourself another date. You are getting too damn handy for me."

There were long, painful evenings in the North Shore Arms with Mary Lou openly flirting with other men while Henry waited on her like a hurt pup. He no longer cared about anything but Mary Lou, arriving home exhausted, he made no attempt to return to the role Laura Jean and his father were waiting on. On days when Mary Lou denied him, he sought her in his sleep, bolting upright in bed to face his wife's hostile stare.

"Was I talking in my sleep? Must have been having a nightmare. It's those ballast tanks. The air we breathe is bad. No oxygen. The language they use, it must get into my brain," he explained weakly. "You say I was talking like that? About sex?" To which Laura Jean would turn away without answering or revealing what she had heard. At these times Henry would push himself out of bed, sweat soaked and weary, and retreat into the bathroom until he could hear his wife's measured breathing.

When he was certain she was asleep, he would slip back into bed to lie staring into the dark, afraid to return to his dreams.

As the summer wound down, Henry became more and more morose with Mary Lou flirting her way around his every attempt to get close. He began cursing in foul language, ceased showering in the morning, arriving in the yards unshaven, sinking deeper each day into the character he hoped would become one of her world. Laura Jean and his father watched, anxiously waiting for September and Henry's return to the man they remembered beneath his summer facade.

August was a time of nothing but misery for Henry. Mary Lou alternated between pouting disinterest and moments of torturing him like a thirsty man in search of a drink. At the end of the first week in September, following an overtime Saturday shift, the crew was notified they were to be back in the yard Sunday to report on the second shift. It meant there would be barely twelve hours between shifts, yet Mary Lou insisted the crew head up Lonsdale to the North Shore Arms for the last hour before closing. Henry trailed after her, arriving home at two in the morning, too tired to wash or to search for his pajamas. He stripped off his coveralls, climbed into bed naked, and left his clothes strewn across the bedroom floor. He remembered only Laura Jean's indignantly twisting in the sheets to escape his presence before he buried his head in the pillow.

He was awakened from a fitful sleep to the sound of the front door of the house closing loudly, conscious only to the fact that there had been no preliminary ringing of the doorbell.

"Hellooo. Anybody home in this house?"

It was his father's voice, intended as a pleasant, enquiring greeting, but penetrating the bedroom like a call to judgment. Henry buried his head deeper into the pillow. The old man called again and Laura Jean wrapped herself in her dressing gown and went out into the hall. Henry lay as if dead, his head wrapped in the pillow.

"Missed you at service this morning." The old man's statement was clearly an accusation, with an explanation fully expected.

Laura Jean stood facing him in the dimly lit hallway, nervously rubbing her hands over her thighs. "Henry is still in bed." She was not about to make even a pretense of defending him.

"In bed? It's past noon. Come, come now." The old man's voice rose incredulously.

Laura Jean shrugged.

"He's not sick? Because if he's not sick, he's going to make himself sick lying around in bed all Sunday morning."

"He didn't get home until after one o'clock," Laura Jean said and opened the bedroom door. "It's your father, Henry. He's here."

The elder Calder pushed past her into the bedroom. Henry sat up, wondering in that moment if traces of Mary Lou's fingernail scars of passion were visible on his adulterated flesh. He had rejoiced at her tearing with her nails at his back, delighting in the evidence of her physical claim on his body. The sheet fell away to expose his groin, the sight of which brought a gasp from Laura Jean. She had a fleeting thought that the old man would assume they slept naked and that she had inflicted the wounds clearly visible on Henry's exposed shoulders. Only once in their entire marriage had she felt the wiry, electrical hairs of Henry's body on her skin. The shock had transformed their coupling into a twisting, pulling struggle through a veneer of cotton pajamas and nightgowns. Henry started to cover himself, then rejected the impulse.

"What's he want?" he demanded of Laura Jean without turning to look at his father. "Didn't you tell him I was sleeping?" The small room suddenly grew even smaller.

"What is the matter with you, son?" the elder Calder demanded.

"It's his work," Laura Jean mumbled. "The shipyard is quite debilitating for him." The father nodded skeptically.

"I'll wait in the living room while he gets dressed," he said petulantly.

"Wait? Wait 'till hell freezes over, as far as I'm concerned." Henry heard his own voice shouting as if he were listening to another person. "Dammit, I'm tired. Can't anyone understand that?" He was hollering loud enough to be heard out in the street. "I try and get a little sleep between shifts and the whole damn world comes marching in here." He's resentment at the presence of the austere figure in the doorway had escaped and Henry had no will to contain it any longer.

Laura Jean saw the elder Calder's face drawn with rage and she felt a momentary surge of compassion for the old man. She was noticing for the first time the stoop to his shoulders and the shaking of his heavily veined hands. A degree of her deference toward his authority had vanished with Henry's outburst.

"I will make us some tea," she said softly, her loose lower lip trembling uncertainly in disbelief. She looked on the stranger in her bed and felt as if the ten years of their carefully structured life together had vanished. "Tea always seems to bring Henry around when he has had a hard night at the yards," she added.

Once in the hallway beyond the bedroom door the old man wheeled on her. "What's the matter in this house," he demanded. "Why can't my boy speak civilly to his father? What is going on between you two? Why have you not consulted me about this condition?" His voice dropped to a gossip whisper. "Laura Jean. Are you...are you denying him his physical needs? Is that it?"

"He's just tired," she answered testily.

The two of them sat together in the musty little living room without bothering to raise the window blinds to the early afternoon, the old man cradling his hat on his lap, a cup of tepid tea growing cold in his hands, both of them awaiting the sound of a stirring from the bedroom.

Henry knew they were there and remained wrapped in the bed covers, marveling at his emancipation. He felt indestructible, his thoughts conjuring a picture of Mary Lou coming into the old man's life. 'Great god. What would the old bugger think about Mary Lou? What if he put those boney hands of his on her ass? Pat her ass, firm as a peach, Father. Take a handful.' Henry smiled at the mental picture of his father groping after Mary Lou. 'Try it, Father. Do it every day until you want to cry and never let go.'

Henry emerged from the bedroom late in the afternoon. The weather had turned to rain, the damp, cold air seeming to fill the sitting room with a chilled silence. He raised the window blinds without acknowledging his father and went to the telephone in the hall. In a voice intended as much for his father as it was for the operator, he asked information for the telephone number of H.L. Kronkite's home.

"Hello, Harold Kronkite? This is Henry Calder, yes, Henry Calder. I'm phoning to inform you that I will not be returning to school this fall. That's right. I'm staying on at the shipyard. I don't know for how long. As long as there is a war on, I suppose." There was a brief muffled conversation that didn't carry into the living room and Henry hung up the phone. He turned to face the stunned silence in the sitting room. The elder Calder appeared to have been frozen in his chair, his eyes wide with astonishment, his face ashen.

"I won't have it, Henry. You can't be serious." The old man's hat fell to the floor. Laura Jean scrambled to retrieve it. "Your work. Your career." Laura Jean sighed heavily, handed the old man his hat, and he got up and left the room.

The rain that had begun about noon developed into a near torrent by the time Henry Calder arrived at the harbor landing for the North Shore ferry. A stiff wind blowing in off the Gulf of Georgia cut through his rain jacket, driving the rain into his face and running down his neck. He felt hot and tired as he looked across the inlet to the yard, a maze of twinkling lights that outlined the vast, hulking shadows of the hulls drawn up on the shore. Henry shrugged deeper into his jacket and sought shelter behind a telephone booth as the ferry nudged into the dock. He was looking for Mary Lou among the surge of shift workers flooding in through the ferry gate when Mary Lou appeared, swept along in the mass of bodies fanning out through the ferry gate, and then disappeared in the crowd.

The work went badly that night until the dinner break when Mary Lou recklessly tossed the last of her bucket of hot rivets over the ship's side into the water. Henry seized her arm before she could leave the deck.

"Mary Lou, I'm sorry about the way I acted. What I'm trying to say is, I can't go on with us being like this. With you upset."

"If you must know Hank, what's bothering me has nothing to do with you. I have a problem of my own, so forget it, eh." She looked directly at him, her words coming in the pouting voice of an unhappy child. After a moment with neither of them stirring, she added petulantly. "I need money, Hank. I need it right now. And I don't have time to be worrying about you or anybody else."

"Money? Then why didn't you say so?" From deep within his hidden fantasies there was the immediate thought that she was pregnant. He had done it. In his fumbling, sophomoric lovemaking he had knocked her up. The idea exploded across his mind. An abortion. She needed an abortion. Marriage. He couldn't check the possibilities that came tumbling one after the other through his mind as he clung to her arm in the rain. "Are you pregnant?" The question blurted out without bidding.

"You must be nuts," she said with a look of disgust. "I need money, that's all." They were alone on the open deck, the wind snapping at their clothes. Mary Lou was dirt-smeared, her hair rain-slicked to her skull, the harsh deck light carving deep shadows in her face. Henry took off his coat and placed it over her shoulders.

"Anything I have is yours, Mary Lou, you know that. Only," he stammered, "can't I be included in what's happening?"

Her voice rose irritably.

"I just spelled it out for you, Hank. I need money. What more do you need to know? Dough. Moola. Get it? I have a problem."

"Okay, sweetheart, okay. You don't have to explain. It's only that I want to share whatever it is that's got you so upset." He fished into his coveralls and pulled out his wallet.

"Hank, I don't want your change," she said with an exasperated sigh. "I need real money. So, forget it. Forget I even mentioned it."

"How much real money?"

"Two hundred," she said as if she were quoting the time of day to a man shaking his watch in disbelief.

"Two hundred dollars?" Henry's jaw dropped.

"Oh, hell, Hank." She shrugged free of his coat and it dropped to the wet steel as she ducked down the hatch steps to where the others were eating in the shelter below deck.

The second half of the shift ground slowly through the hours to midnight. Henry attacked each rivet with a vicious determination while Mary Lou slammed the hot slugs in place, neither of them attempting to speak a word. Henry was replaying her words over again and again in his mind, slowly shaping a plan. Finally he had it, an idea that would make everything right. She was, after all, a woman. It was so obvious. Why had he not reasoned this out in the beginning? Confident he had discovered what it was that would solve any problem, he laughed softly to himself, ridiculing himself for not having seen the answer in the first place. When the shift whistle brought a halt to the work on deck, Mary Lou went for her bucket. Henry stood in her way, grinning apologetically.

"Mary Lou." He swallowed a surge of protective passion in his voice. "I have something to say to you. Something important, to both of us." She raised her eyebrows indifferently, her expression mystically alluring in the shadows of the deck lights. "Let's go someplace where we can talk? Where it's quiet?" He fought to overcome the pleading tone creeping into his voice. He wanted to go down on his knees before her, wrap his arms around her legs, show that he was hers. All hers.

"This is as quiet as it gets Hank." Mary Lou said quietly and waved an arm across the glistening, rain-swept deck. "Let's have it."

"Mary Lou, will you marry me?" He saw her eyes open like camera shutters seeking images in the dark. There was a moment of stunned silence. Henry took a deep breath, more certain each moment that she didn't speak that he had been right. "I'm going to get a divorce," he added hurriedly. "I know, all married men say that. But I really am. You don't know what's been happening to me at home. It's all over for me there, Mary Lou. Ever since we first met, it's been over. You and I will get married, I give you my word." He was unable to catch his breath, caught up in the wonder of his own words, words so startling they sounded unreal. "Mary Lou, it is time you and I got married."

"To each other?" Henry could barely hear her whispered response.

"That's right. You and me. Man and wife forever. We will make our own friends. We will create our own world, together." He was cherishing each syllable, proclaimed his intentions as if he were sharing a vision in the night. "Whatever I have is yours. My entire outlook has been wrong from the beginning. I was acting just like all the other men in your life. I know that now. All I thought of was your body. Our love is bigger than that, Mary Lou. We are made for one another. Every day, every night, side by side for the rest of our lives. You need never be alone again, dearest."

For an instant the thought occurred to her that he had lost his mind. They were alone, sixty feet above the ground on an open deck. She glanced over her shoulder hoping one of the others was still on the deck. Seeing no one, she stepped back, cautiously.

"Hank. I don't want to marry you."

The wild excitement on his face slowly fell away, leaving an expression that resembled a slaughter-house cow that had just been struck between the horns by the butcher's sledge hammer.

"What's so hard to understand, Hank? "

"What is it you want me to do, then?" he asked submissively. "We can just live together, if that's the way you want things. Forget marriage. It means nothing to people who are in love." He was grasping for the thread that would check his unraveling dream. He had it a moment ago. Now it was slipping away. He reached for her hands. "The miracle is, we have found one another in this place. This hell hole of war and steel and noise and foul shit. And we found each other." His voice faded away as she pulled her hands free.

"Mary Lou. Believe me. I am offering you my life, my career. Everything I have is yours." He wanted to croon the words, to make them sound like they sounded on the record on the North Arms jukebox.

"How much money do you have?" When she spoke, he detected a new interest, a softness to her voice.

His mind went to the savings book. "Seven, nearly eight hundred dollars," he answered in a deflated voice. "It's for the car."

"Okay, Hank. Everybody needs a car." She turned to leave. "A car will be nice for you and your wife. You can also get your pussy there, my friend." He started after her through the long shadows between the half-built hulls, trotting like an unsure dog trailing an uncertain meal, his short steps echoing in the hollow beneath his feet. The cool, dank air from the stinking beach exposed by low tide enveloped him in a death-like depression that made it difficult to move.

A sane voice, an echo of someone he had been in the past, began to scold. 'Get hold of yourself, Henry Calder. The bitch is making a bloody fool of you. Kiss the dame goodbye. Be done with her. Au revoir, mademoiselle. For God's sake, the money is not yours. Half of the money belongs to Laura Jean. Your father has put his pension money into that pot. Think man. Think about all her other men. You know she never learned those tricks playing with you? Marry her? You would be out of your mind.' It was the solid Henry in ascendency who was trailing after her through the yard gate.

'There is something decent in life for you Henry. You have a future. This is forty-year-old madness. This is an experience. Thank God that you got hold of yourself in time. You have been crazy. Crazy as hell.' He watched Mary Lou continue through the gate, her head tilted defiantly as she tucked her time card into the clock. Henry passed the clock, ignoring his card and the timekeeper behind the window.

"Hey, mister," the timekeeper pressed his lips to the opening in the glass. "You don't get paid if you don't punch out." If the timekeeper's call reached his ears, it didn't slow his pace as he began to hurry. His inner voice calling him back to sanity sounded less certain.

'You are a man of decent breeding, Henry. Pay for that woman and you are nothing more than a whore chaser. Another fifteen years at Hudson School and you have a pension for life. Write. Teach. The world has a role for you, with your pants on.'

Mary Lou stopped at the ferry ramp and turned to face the blank confusion in his eyes, looking at him as if she were facing a stranger. Henry forced a smile. He knew that if he boarded the ferry with her, she would get off and go back up the hill to the North Shore Arms.

"Goodbye, Hank," she said, the mockery in her voice and eyes bringing tears to his cheeks. His inner voice took on the slang of the character he had shaped in the yard.

'Fool? Who's a fool? You have been fooling yourself for forty years, Henry. That gal has brought

life to you, you sorry prick. She stuck her finger up
your ass and you came alive, boy. That woman made
love to you with belly sucking sweat. Yeah, Henry,
take a bite outta that woman and you shall be turned
out of the garden, eh. Okay. Turn me out. I always
wanted to live like a god.'

"Mary Lou." He reached out to take her by the
shoulder. "I can get you the money." He spoke in
his own voice, the weak voice of the Henry Calder
he knew she had uncovered in him. "Tomorrow."

"Two hundred?"

Henry nodded silently.

Mary Lou smiled, a warm, forgiving smile, and
pushed the wet hair from her face. "Okay, Hank.
Then come on, I'll let you buy me a ten-cent beer."

 From the moment he awoke the following
morning, Henry moved with the step of a man
approaching his own damnation. He slipped out of
bed and dressed quietly. Before leaving the
bedroom, he went to the drawer containing his
teaching certificate, his wife's costume jewelry, and
the savings book. He was so quiet going through the
drawer that Laura Jean, with her eyes closed faking
sleep until he was gone, did not hear nor suspect. He
removed the book, reassuring himself that if he was
indeed stealing, he was stealing from himself,
accepting that as reinforcement of his decision to
severe his past.

Henry arrived outside the cigar store at the
corner of Hastings and Richards Streets fifteen
minutes before the bank opened. He was also fifteen
minutes ahead of the schedule Mary Lou had set and

began pacing up and down the block, his nerves jumping with each metallic shriek of the passing streetcar wheels biting into the corner tracks. Mary Lou was on time. She had dressed for the occasion in a snug, imitation fur jacket, her dark hair set with an artificial pink flower. As Henry watched her step down from the motorman's compartment of the Kingsway streetcar, the steep step to the street appeared to lift her tight skirt above her knees, revealing her thigh and the top of her rolled silk stockings. What she saw on his face told her she had done right in coming spiffy.

"Am I late?" There was a childish anticipation in her question. Henry shot an anxious glance up and down the sidewalk and steered her to the cigar store doorway.

"Bank doesn't open until nine thirty," he whispered.

She squeezed him around the waist and pushed him back out onto the sidewalk, her eyes alive with mischief. "Then we can window shop," she whispered.

Standing in the midst of the morning traffic with Mary Lou's arm around his waist, Henry was suddenly conscious of his lunch pail hanging awkwardly from his hand. He had packed it the night before so as not to arouse Laura Jean's suspicion. He wished now he had left the pail on the tram seat. He would have thrown it into the gutter if he could have done so inconspicuously. Mary Lou pulled him closer and kissed his cheek. Henry flushed, certain he was being watched by everyone on Hastings Street, but he didn't try to stop her.

"Mary Lou, I better go into the bank alone," he said, continuing his conspiratorial whisper. "There's no point in giving them any more cause to talk than we are already." He saw the disappointment in her eyes. "It's just to keep you out of trouble, in case."

"In case? In case of what? It's your money isn't it?"

"Not so loud. Yes. It is, mostly my money."

Her lips puckered in a childish pout. "Well, if you are ashamed of me, Hank."

"For crying out loud, Mary Lou, there are people in the bank who could go running to Laura Jean or to my father." He was remembering the assistant manager whose desk fronted on the bank lobby and also served as the Cathedral treasurer.

"Henry. Hank." Mary Lou interrupted his thought with a pixie-like voice and placed the tip of her fingers to his lips. "Get two hundred and fifty."

"Two fifty? You said..."

"So we can have some to spend. We want lunch and maybe a place to play awhile, eh."

"A place to play?"

"A room."

Henry was certain the teller, a middle-aged, big-nosed woman who fancied herself an ambassador of the bank's good will, knew everything the moment he stepped up to the window. Henry could see it written all over her face. To Henry, it seemed that she was peering out at him through the cage window with a look that fairly shouted 'I know what you are up to, Henry Calder.' He was her first customer.

"I want two hundred and fifty dollars," he blurted. The teller's fixed smile held and her eyes went to the passbook.

"You mean you are withdrawing?" She looked up expecting a conversational explanation. Henry half expected she was about to tell him he would regret what he was doing.

"It's my money," he snapped.

"I guess you deserve it by now," the woman replied awkwardly. "I mean, this is your first withdrawal since, let's see, in three years."

Nosey damn bitch. Henry silently cursed himself for having chosen her window. The teller filled out a withdrawal slip and passed it to him to sign. "It makes saving worthwhile when we can put it to good use, isn't it?" the woman remarked, fishing for a story that would fit her concept of saving to complete a dream. Henry didn't answer and he didn't count the bills she handed him nor did he stop to read where she had posted the new balance in the passbook.

His hands were shaking when he met Mary Lou on the curb and counted out ten of the twenty-dollar bills and handed them to her. One of the remaining twenties slipped through his fingers and fluttered to the sidewalk. Before he could reach for it, Mary Lou nailed it to the sidewalk with the heel of her patent leather pump. She bent over, her soft woolen skirt rising over her hips, and slipped the twenty into her purse with the others.

"That one's for luck, Hank. You will see. You are going to get your money's worth." He couldn't erase the thought that in less than two minutes out of the bank, he had thirty dollars left from the two hundred and fifty.

Mary Lou chose the hotel, a tired-looking storefront facing Denman Street, the hotel's store plate-glass windows exposing the lobby to the passing pedestrians. Henry nervously turned his back to the street as the clerk pushed the register across the desk. Mary Lou sidled up to him with a reassuring smile and Henry signed his name hurriedly in an illegible scrawl.

"That'll be fourteen dollars, in advance." The clerk dangled the room key tantalizingly over the desk. Henry handed him one of his remaining twenties and snatched the key and his change. He followed Mary Lou to the elevator, fixing his eyes on her hips jiggling beneath the wool skirt, hoping to calm his nerves. The cage doors on the elevator closed behind them and they rose, still exposed to the lobby. She turned and pressed her wet lips to his mouth, leaving a taste of peppermint candy. Over her shoulder, Henry saw the desk clerk's eyes following the cage as it disappeared between floors. The clerk was laughing.

"Is it against the law to register with a false name?" he whispered anxiously, fixing the key into the door lock.

"What do you think it is to take a girl into a hotel room for what we are going to do?" she answered with a mischievous elbow to his ribs.

"You mean for money?" There was no malice in the remark. It had just popped loose but he knew he had made a mistake even before she wheeled on him with venom in her voice.

"What the hell's that supposed to mean?"

"Mary Lou, it didn't mean anything. I don't know much about this business. Don't be angry and spoil it." He pulled the door shut behind him and reached out to put his arm around her waist.

"Hands off." She twisted away. "I'm not bought and paid for, no matter what you think."

Mary Lou undressed without speaking and lay on the bed without removing her blue satin brassiere. She served him swiftly, without passion, leaving him disconsolate and empty while she fussed with her hair before the dressing table mirror. Henry lay back and closed his eyes, attempting to escape the iron poster bed and the musty hotel room. It was mid-morning and he felt trapped, his clothes strewn across the floor with Mary Lou sulking and puffing angrily on a cigarette.

He must have slept, for his next recollection was of her body, warm and damp next to him on the bed, and she was kissing him with a lustiness that awakened his urge to possess her again. She held him this time, insistently, far beyond the limits of his own passion. Henry lay watching as Mary Lou slept through the afternoon, her deep breathing puckering her lips so deliciously he had to restrain himself from placing his mouth on hers. As the shadows moved across the room, he cautiously moved from the bed, arching his back in an attempt to loosen the pain that had struck during their lovemaking. When he retrieved his trousers from the floor and searched the pockets for what was left of his money, he counted sixteen dollars and eighty cents.

***

It all ended Monday morning three weeks later. Laura Jean had slipped out of bed before dawn and began creeping about the bedroom in the dark, attempting to gather up her clothes without awakening Henry. When she opened the bedroom door to step into the hall, the hall light revealed Henry's coveralls and work boots scattered about the room. Laura Jean hesitated before stepping back into the bedroom and began gathering his things off the bedroom floor. The bank savings book dropped from the pocket of his coveralls.

Slowly, she turned the pages as if she were peeling away a painful bandage, her eyes tracing the record of withdrawals until she came to the remaining balance. Seven dollars and eighty cents. She looked over at Henry's crumpled form twisted and knotted in the bedclothes, the shadows from the hall making the bed and his shape appear like a pile of dirty laundry. Without waking him, she went into the living room and telephoned his father.

Henry never pulled his head out from the covers all the time his father stood shouting over the bed. Only when the old man sounded as if he had run out of breath did Henry raise his head to glance wearily about the room.

"I have a mind to call the police," the old man shouted, the spittle on his lips spraying with the energy of his indignation. He waved the passbook in Henry's face. "You have been stealing from me, your own father." Getting no response, he turned on Laura Jean. "Those were my pension dollars. I gave every dime I had to spare just so that you could have the car. And you and that boy have repaid me with your thievery." The old man's voice rose to a near scream, the veins in his neck pulsing with anger. "You are equally to blame for what has happened to my son, you are part of this, I know."

Silently, without looking at the old man, Laura Jean went to the bedroom dresser and began packing her clothes into a suitcase. Henry and his father watched in silence until she went out the front door. The following morning a real estate agent arrived and informed Henry the house had been listed for sale. It had been bought with her money, money from her streetcar motorman father who had insisted it be in Laura Jean's name.

Over the weeks that followed, the once-tidy brown house with the neatly clipped grass and crisp crinoline curtains became a rat warren, the bed unmade, the sink stacked with dirty dishes, the garbage of Henry's winter alone strewn in every room. He slept in his work clothes and began to smell, so that the crew avoided him even in the open air above decks.

Henry never returned to the classroom. The last the elderly Calder heard from his son was a postcard from Montreal, long after the war. Henry had scribbled a note asking him to send money in care of the YMCA, promising to repay him when he found work.

###

Old Folks' Romance

She was seventy-five years old and her husband had been dead seven years and it was Sunday, the third Sunday in a row the kids hadn't shown up. A chill filled the apartment despite the late afternoon sunlight slanting across the carpet, slowly slipping down the far wall. She thought about the television, but the gray, lifeless tube, like everything else in the room, offered little that would ease the loneliness. She thought again of calling him.

After all, it was he who had approached her. He had even given her his number, in case she changed her mind. He had been standing by the mailbox in the hallway and spoke to her as she stepped out of the elevator. "Hello. Have you seen the mailman?"

She had intended to not notice him. Nice ladies, nice old ladies, don't notice strange men loitering in the hallway. Her glance went to the soup stain on his sweater, then to the gray stubble sprouting from his chin. He hadn't shaved. Nothing about him was like Monty; certainly no gentleman like her Monty.

"It's Sunday." The hostility in her voice startled her. He smiled, revealing a tooth missing on one side of his mouth. There was something vulnerable in that smile that made her regret having answered so sharply.

He shook his head apologetically. "I lose track of what day it is. Every day seems the same. I guess it's the rain or the gray days. I kinda lose interest. You out for a walk?"

"No. I'm waiting for my daughter." In a way it was true, only she was now sure Jessica was not coming. Why not say yes? That's what you had in mind when you put on your coat. Once around the block. She tried guessing his age. It's harder with a man, especially when he hasn't shaved. A trace of color ran through his hair. Maybe sixty-five, seventy? Maybe even older, seventy-five. Looks as if he drinks. She tried to silence the bitter, silent voice whispering in her head. It had been a long time since she had a drink with a man.

"Guess I'll have to go alone," he said. "Don't know this neighborhood. Lived in Seattle most of my life. Knew every block for miles back then. Kids wanted me to come live here, so's they could keep an eye on me."

"You mean so they could visit you?"

"That was the idea. I think it was more like they wanted to keep tabs on me." He turned up the collar on his heavy woolen sweater. "Maybe they were afraid I was going to run off and get married again." He laughed easily at himself.

"Were you?" She was suddenly conscious of the fact that she was standing talking to a stranger, asking questions she would hesitate to answer herself. "I mean, did you have someone in mind?"

A long moment passed before he answered. She realized he was looking at her like a man looks at a woman and she felt the warmth rising in her cheeks. Her hair was done right. She had set it in curlers for the children; rinsed it with just a trace of the blue tint Jessica said made her look cheap.

"No." He laughed again, a soft, intimate chuckle. "Been living alone too long for that." The elevator remained open. She was no longer maintaining the pretence of having to hurry away. "Come on," he said. "Walk with me. I might get lost on my own. Once around the block. We can keep an eye out for your kids." He pushed open the door. Jessica's not showing up no longer seemed important.

There was a bite in the late afternoon wind, and for a time they said nothing. Then he began to softly sing an old country music hall tune.

"Around the corner and under the trees.

The sergeant major, made love to me.

He kissed me once. He kissed me twice.

It wasn't just the thing to do, but gosh it was so nice."

"You were in the service?" she asked.

"First War. We used to call it the World War, until they started the next one."

"You must have been just a boy."

"Sixteen. Told 'em I was seventeen. Biggest mistake of my life," he answered and smiled quietly, as if he enjoyed the joke.

"Your parents let you do that ?"

"Dad was a streetcar motorman and a milk truck driver at the same time. Didn't have time to know what his ten kids were doing."

"Ten?"

"He blamed it all on the Pope."

This time she laughed. The sound of her voice startled her for the second time that day.

"You are Catholic?"

"Well," he answered uncertainly. "The church may not think so. But I go when I have something I need to talk over with the man upstairs."

"I have often envied Catholics with their sense of close proximity to God. I can't imagine where you get the faith to conceive that your bread and wine are what they say they are."

"Mostly, we pray for it. Faith, I mean."

She grew silent for a moment.

"And the idols. I went into one of your churches, the big one up on Tenth Avenue for a funeral of a friend of Monty's. There were idols everywhere with candles and people praying in front of them."

He laughed. "You better not get me started. I'm probably a bigger agnostic than you have ever been. Who's Monty?"

"My late husband."

He nodded quietly, fitting the information in with what he knew of her.

"Those must have been difficult days," she said.

"What?"

"When your father held two jobs. My Monty went out at night selling insurance door to door. He had to, with the cost of keeping our kids in school. We owned a penny candy store on Fourth Avenue. Some months there wasn't enough to pay the store rent."

"When did he die?"

"We lost him two years ago."

"Lost him? You mean you really lost him?"

"It was his heart. He was shaving one morning. Dropped the razor. I got the shaving cream all over my blouse when I tried to get him to sit up. The doctor said he was probably gone when he hit the floor."

"Oh. You mean you lost him when he died."

She looked puzzled. "What did you think...?"

"It sounded like he wandered off." He smiled apologetically.

They were back at the apartment door, and he was awkwardly rubbing the chill from his hands. "I guess I'll go pour myself a hot toddy. Get the chill out of my bones," he said. "How about you. Are you interested?"

"It's been nice," she said, suddenly afraid Jessica would arrive late. Jessica couldn't handle finding her in a man's room. He stepped closer, slowly so that she had time to put her hand out and stop him before anything happened. He was going to kiss her. She knew that. It was like when she was a girl and the boys were so awkward. He had the awkwardness of a young boy.

She picked up the phone.

###

About the Author

Gerry Pratt wrote for the *Toronto Telegram*, while it still existed, and *The Globe and Mail* in Toronto, Ontario, as well as *The Vancouver Sun* in British Columbia. He was fired from *The Seattle Times* because he misspelled Syracuse. He finally ended up at *The Oregonian*, where he wrote the column 'Making The Dollar.' Additionally, *The Oregonian* assignments took him to most parts of the world and many of the eventual wars of the late twentieth century. He is the youngest of a family of eleven children.

Gerry's other books include *God is Blue and other short stories*, *Love Never Dies*, *In Search of a Hero*, and *The Merchants*.